VOYAGERS

TOP-SECRET MISSION BRIEF

PROJECT ALPHA

YOU HAVE BEEN CHOSEN

Humankind is facing the threat of extinction, and we need YOUR help to keep the world from going dark.

Join the Voyagers team now and log in to **VoyagersHQ.com** to receive your Top-Secret Mission Assignment. We need you to build your custom ZRK commander, collect and train ZRK squads, and explore the depths of space.

FAILURE IS NOT AN OPTION.

Shawn Phillips

Commanding Officer | Voyagers Program | Base Ten

Eight finalists have been chosen.

Only four will win the chance to voyage to the far end of the galaxy and back.

And I will be their guide.

STEAM 6000

PROJECT ALPHA

D. J. MacHale

Random House New York

To all the loyal members of The Little Click Club

 Published in the United States by
Random House Children's Books,
a division of Penguin Random House LLC, New York.

Visit us on the Web! randomhousekids.com

Educators and librarians, for a variety of teaching tools,
visit us at RHTeachersLibrarians.com

VoyagersHQ.com

Library of Congress Cataloging-in-Publication Data
MacHale, D. J.
Project Alpha / D.J. MacHale.—First edition.
pages cm.—(Voyagers ; book 1)
Summary: Eight boys and girls compete for a spot on the space voyage
that will search for a source to solve Earth's energy crisis.
ISBN 978-0-385-38658-6 (trade)—ISBN 978-0-385-38660-9 (lib. bdg.)
ISBN 978-0-385-38659-3 (ebook)
[1. Interplanetary voyages—Fiction. 2. Competition (Psychology)—Fiction.
3. Power resources—Fiction. 4. Science fiction.] I. Title.
PZ7.M177535Pr 2015 [Fic]—dc23 2014031772

Printed in the United States of America
10 9 8 7 6 5 4 3 2 1
First Edition

Random House Children's Books supports the
First Amendment and celebrates the right to read.

PART ONE

BASE TEN

1

Dark.

Pitch-dark.

The kind where you can't tell if you're next to a thousand other people, standing totally alone . . .

. . . or about to step off a cliff.

"We should stay close," Dash Conroy said, his voice echoing in the vast empty space.

"I'm fine on my own," Anna Turner replied curtly.

Anna wasn't about to show weakness or fear, especially not in front of Dash. There was too much at stake. This was a competition she was determined to win.

"We can help each other," Dash argued. "At least until we figure out what the real challenge is."

Their assignment was clear: retrieve the golden flag. Whoever got it first would be the winner. Simple, except navigating their way through the darkness wasn't their only task. Something else would be waiting for them. An obstacle. A puzzle. A test.

Danger was out there. They both knew it.

They just couldn't see it.

"I'm gonna shuffle ahead slowly," Dash said. "If I hit something, I'll let you know."

"If you hit something, I'll hear it," Anna shot back.

Walking into the unknown had Dash's stomach in a knot. There was no way to know if there was a hundred yards of nothing between him and the golden flag or if he was inches away from something sharp waiting to skewer him.

"Are you behind me?" Dash asked, trying not to let his voice crack with tension.

"Why? You nervous?" Anna asked coyly. "Maybe you should sit this one out."

"No, I'm okay— Ow!"

Dash pulled his hands back quickly.

"What is it?" Anna asked anxiously.

"I hit something." He tentatively put his hands out to discover a smooth, flat surface. "It feels like a tall desk. There's a flat top and . . . uh-oh."

"What?" Anna asked.

"I think it's a control panel," Dash said with growing excitement. "This could be how to turn the lights on."

"No!" Anna screamed in Dash's ear, making him jump with surprise.

"Whoa! Why not?"

"What if it's a trap? Those switches could electrify the floor. Or open up a canyon we can't jump over. Or—"

"Or it could turn on the lights," Dash said calmly. "If something's out there, we have to see it."

Dash put one finger on each of the switches and flipped them.

Instantly, powerful overhead lights kicked on, illuminating the giant space to reveal they were inside a massive, eight-story-high white tent. Dash was right. Turning on the lights allowed them to see what was out there.

It was a fifty-foot-tall dinosaur with a long snout filled with multiple rows of teeth. Sharp teeth.

The two stood looking up at the beast in wide-eyed, stunned amazement.

"Oh, that's not good," Anna said, dumbfounded.

The monster reared back and let out a chilling bellow that shook the overhead lighting grid.

"Move!" Dash yelled, and pushed her behind a pile of wooden crates next to the control panel.

"I told you not to flip those switches," Anna said in a strained whisper.

"Seriously?" Dash whispered back. "You'd rather we just walked into that thing?"

"It's a dinosaur! Why is there a dinosaur?"

Dash peered around the edge of the crates to see the behemoth clawing at the floor with its huge, birdlike feet, scraping the surface with lethal talons. It stood in the center of the giant tent, thirty yards away, twisting its head one way and then the other like a curious dog that just heard a strange sound.

"What's it doing?" Anna whispered.

"It seems bothered," Dash replied.

Dash raised his hand. Strapped to his wrist was a wide, flexible band that held a small, flat computer monitor. His fingers moved quickly over the soft touch pad that covered most of his forearm until an image appeared on the small screen. It was an exact drawing of the creature.

"That's it!" Anna said, staring at the image over Dash's shoulder.

"It's a Raptogon," Dash said, reading the info. "It eats meat."

"Of course it does."

"It's got a superior sense of smell and can run up to thirty miles an hour," Dash read. "But it has poor peripheral vision and is ultra sensitive to bright light."

The Raptogon let out another bellow. Dash stole a quick peek to see that the animal was bobbing its head and chuffing angrily.

"What's happening?" Anna asked.

"I think the lights are bothering it."

"Perfect," Anna said sarcastically. "An angry carnivorous monster."

Dash scanned the rest of the vast space, calculating their next move. There were random stacks of wooden crates scattered throughout the tent, which could be used to hide behind, but running from one to the next would leave them exposed to the predator. On the far side of the huge tent, nearly a hundred yards away, was a raised platform with the golden flag hanging from a pole. That was the target. Whichever of them got to it first would win the challenge.

"There's a locker," Dash said, pointing.

Anna looked to see a coffin-sized container lying flat, twenty yards to their right.

"They must have put something in there to help us," Dash said. "Like a weapon."

"Man, that thing's big," Anna said, staring at the fidgety creature.

They both sat back behind the crates.

"We can't outrun it," Dash said. "But maybe it can be distracted. Let's work together."

"No," Anna said sharply. "This is a contest."

"It's about getting that flag," Dash shot back. "I don't think either of us can do that alone."

Anna stared straight into Dash's eyes, calculating her next move.

"All right," she said flatly. "But I don't take orders from anybody."

"I won't give you any. I just want to get the flag and not get eaten in the—"

A dark shadow slipped over them, blocking out the light. They both slowly looked up to see the head of the Raptogon looming above them.

Dash instantly scrambled backward, knocking over the crates that had been their screen. The wooden boxes tumbled like dice at the feet of the dinosaur, forcing the beast to dance out of the way.

Anna was already up and running for the locker. Dash scrambled to his feet and was right after her. Anna got there first, threw it open, and peered inside.

"Nothing!" she exclaimed. "No weapons."

Dash arrived and looked inside. "No, this is good!" he exclaimed.

Inside were two high-powered flashlights with six-inch lenses.

"It's sensitive to light," he added, breathless. He grabbed

both and handed one to Anna. "We'll hit its eyes from both sides. Whichever way it turns, it'll be blinded and we can work our way to the flag."

Anna looked back to the Raptogon. It had regained its balance and was scanning for them.

"You sure about this?" she said, showing a rare hint of uncertainty.

"Yes," Dash replied calmly. "It has bad lateral movement, so keep moving to the side."

The Raptogon zeroed in on the two, shrieked, and charged. Its massive claws pounded the floor as it stormed toward its prey.

Dash quickly pressed the button on his flashlight and a powerful beam of white light shot out.

"I'll go left; you go right," Dash said, and darted away.

The Raptogon bared its teeth. Somebody was about to get chewed.

Dash hit it in the face with the light beam.

The monster immediately stopped and let out a hideous screech that made the hair on Dash's neck stand up.

"Hit it!" Dash screamed to Anna.

Anna turned on her flashlight and aimed it at the Raptogon's face.

The massive creature snapped its head from side to side as if trying to shake off the painful light.

"It's working!" Dash exclaimed. "Keep moving to the side."

Dash moved laterally, doing his best to keep the light focused on the Raptogon's sensitive eyes.

The beast pounded at the ground in pain and anger, and charged for Dash.

"Stay on it!" Dash commanded.

Dash had to run for his life. The Raptogon was fighting through the pain to get to its tormentor. It shrieked. It snarled. It shook its head in anguish, but it kept coming.

"Help!" Dash screamed. "Anna! Keep the light on it!"

The beast would not be denied. Dash tried desperately to move out of the charging monster's path, but he was running out of room. The dinosaur had him cornered. Dash banged into a stack of crates, knocking them down and then tripping over the tumbling boxes. He couldn't keep the flashlight steady, and the monster knew it. Again it bared its teeth, sensing the kill.

Dash fell flat on his back. He kicked at the boxes, hoping they might slow the beast down.

They didn't.

He was trapped.

"Anna!" Dash yelled in desperation.

The monster screamed, opened its mouth, lunged at Dash . . .

. . . and vanished.

Dash was left cowering in the corner with his arms over his head for protection.

A harsh horn sounded, signaling the end of the competition.

The Raptogon was a hologram. It may have seemed authentic, but there was never any real danger.

A cheer went up, followed by applause.

Dash slowly lowered his arms to see a group of kids observing the competition from a catwalk high above the floor. Several of them cheered and clapped. Others watched silently. Standing with them was an adult man who was surveying the scene with his hands on his hips.

"We have a winner!" he announced, his amplified words booming through the cavernous space.

Dash wasn't sure what he meant. How could there have been a winner? They had failed miserably and were nearly eaten.

That's when the truth hit him.

He looked to the platform on the far side of the tent to see Anna standing on top, waving the golden flag in triumph.

It was a harsh lesson. He had to be careful about who to trust. It was a mistake he vowed not to make again. That is, as long as he wasn't knocked out of the competition for having lost the golden flag.

Not all of them could win the ultimate prize. The odds had been against Dash from the beginning, but that didn't stop him from giving it a shot.

Project Alpha meant too much.

To him.

To his family.

And to the future of the entire world.

2

Dash stared out of his bedroom window at the dark, empty streets of downtown Orlando, Florida.

It was one week before he and Anna would encounter the Raptogon hologram and a solid year since he had first heard about the Project Alpha competition. The very next day, he would leave to begin the final phase. Hundreds of thousands of kids from all over the world had entered for a chance to become part of the project. He was one of eight finalists. Eventually there would be only four winners. Dash never expected to get that far. He thought he stood a better chance of finding a golden ticket in a Wonka Bar than making the final four.

Yet there he was with a fifty-fifty chance.

"I can't get used to this," Dash's mother said as she entered the room. "When the lights go out, it's like the world dies."

She joined Dash at the window and looked out over the darkened city. No lights glowed from any of the tall buildings. Cars were left to sit until their owners returned the next day when they were allowed to drive again. It was the beginning of the daily eight-hour blackout period that happened all over the country. Electricity and gas service were cut off. Telephone, television, Internet, cell phone, and radio communications were shut down. It was a newly mandated government program with only one purpose:

To conserve energy.

It was estimated that within ten years these temporary blackouts would become permanent and within a hundred years the planet would run out of fossil fuel. *All* fossil fuel. The energy crisis that many feared in theory was no longer a theory.

It was very real and the clock was ticking.

"Do you think they shut down Disney World too?" Dash asked.

"Of course," his mom replied. "They're in this situation just like the rest of us."

"I guess it really is a small world after all," Dash said with a smile.

His mom laughed. Dash liked to make her laugh because it didn't happen often. Not anymore. His dad had died two years before and left his mom to raise Dash and his little sister, Abby, on her own. As tough as it was, they got by. Barely. The growing energy crises always felt like somebody else's problem.

Until the lights started going out.

Dash stared out at the night sky. His unruly brown hair needed a trimming. His skin was pasty pale, which wasn't normal for a kid who lived in Florida, but he had been spending most of his time indoors taking the hundreds of Project Alpha tests. He would rather have been out playing baseball with his friends, but becoming part of Project Alpha was something he desperately wanted.

Now he was on the verge of getting his wish.

"You can still back out," Mrs. Conroy said. "It's not too late."

"Why would I do that?" Dash asked with surprise. "This is the most important thing that's ever happened. I have to go."

Mrs. Conroy nodded. She knew he'd say that. Dash was a special kid. He was so scary smart that he skipped two grades in school. More than that, he was wise beyond his years. His friends always looked to him for answers and he usually had them. Mrs. Conroy worked hard to keep the family afloat but Dash was the rock she relied on when times were tough.

With the city blacked-out, the sky came alive with the light from thousands of sparkling stars. The two sat in the window, focused on the life above, not the darkness below.

"Are you scared?" Mrs. Conroy asked.

"A little."

"It's okay," she said. "I am too. Winning the competition is only the beginning."

"I know," Dash said. "That's not what I'm scared of."

"Then what?"

"I'm scared that I won't win."

Mrs. Conroy put her arm around him.

"One way or another, you're going to help these people. You're going to help *us.* I have no doubt about that."

Dash reached out the window and swept his hand across the sky as if he could brush aside the stars.

"Do you think it's possible?" he asked. "Could the answer be out there?"

"I hope so," she said. "But there's one thing I know for an absolute fact."

"What's that?"

"If it's out there, you'll find it."

Twenty-four hours later, a line of eight black SUVs with dark windows charged along a desolate desert road, kicking up mini tornados of sand. They weren't alone. A military escort of a dozen camouflaged Humvees led the way. Another dozen picked up the rear. In the sky, four Cobra attack helicopters flew in formation, acting as a protective umbrella over the caravan.

The vehicles approached a high chain-link fence that stretched out to either side of the road for miles. There were signs everywhere warning that this was a restricted area. Violators would be subject to arrest . . . or be shot. Not necessarily in that order.

Heavily armed soldiers wearing desert fatigues swung the two gates open and waved the caravan through. Once the cars were inside, the helicopters broke off. Their mission was complete. The cargo had arrived safely.

The cars traveled for another mile until the first buildings appeared like an oasis, revealing a sprawling military base and airfield. Fighter jets lined the long runways. Massive hangars loomed high above the desert floor. One of the huge buildings had its giant doors open, and the caravan turned toward it. The Humvees broke off and the SUVs continued on inside. They rolled to the dead center of the vast empty space and all eight vehicles parked side by side.

Behind them, the enormous hangar doors rolled shut, cutting off the sun and intense heat.

A man stood in the center of the hangar, facing the line-up. He was in his thirties and dressed in a dark blue military jumpsuit. There were no insignias or patches, and with his unkempt boyishly cut hair, he didn't fit the typical military mold.

He gave a curt wave and the car doors opened.

First out were the drivers. They were soldiers wearing desert fatigues. They quickly moved to the back doors, pulled them open, and stood at attention.

Slowly, tentatively, the passengers emerged.

They were kids.

Twelve-year-old kids.

Four boys. Four girls.

They stepped out of the vehicles with caution, gazing around at the enormous building in wonder until they laid eyes on one another. It was the first time they were seeing the other finalists in the Project Alpha competition. Some smiled a silent greeting. Others gave steely glares as they appraised the competition.

Last out was a pale girl with blond hair and blue eyes. Her driver brought a motorized wheelchair up to her door and moved to help her out. The girl waved him off. With a quick flip, she pulled herself out of the SUV and onto her wheels. Without missing a beat, she joined the others.

"Welcome," the man in the jumpsuit declared formally. "Don't be shy. Join me."

The man wasn't cold, but he was all business.

The group slowly gathered and formed a line, shoulder to shoulder, facing him. Everyone fidgeted nervously, waiting for whatever might come next.

"Congratulations," the man said sincerely. "Eight finalists. Down from over seven hundred thousand applicants."

"Who are you?" one girl asked skeptically.

"Hello, Anna," he answered while stepping forward to shake her hand. "My name is Shawn Phillips. Commander Phillips. I'm the leader of Project Alpha. It's time for you to meet one another."

Anna was a dark-skinned girl with a mass of curly hair. She looked challengingly at him through oversized rectangular glasses. "Are you the one picking the final four?" she asked as they shook hands.

"I am," he replied.

"Cool. Just want to know who I've got to impress."

Anna stepped back. Next to her, a slight Asian girl with long dark hair and straight bangs stepped forward.

"Carly Diamond," Phillips announced to the group. *"Konnichiwa youkoso."*

"Arigatou," Carly replied with a slight bow, then added, "You don't need to speak to me in Japanese."

"I know that," Phillips said kindly, then addressed the group. "Everyone here is fluent in English. It's the chosen language of Project Alpha."

"Gabriel Parker," Phillips said, continuing down the line.

A boy with dark skin and a mischievous twinkle in his eyes stepped forward. He stood a head taller than the rest, eye to eye with Phillips. "Yes sir," Gabriel said with authority. "Thanks for the chance."

"Thank you for volunteering."

Gabriel's bright eyes shone with eagerness as he stepped back into line.

"Ravi Chavan," Phillips said, shaking the hand of an Indian boy.

"You got it," Ravi answered with a slight accent and a cocky sort of grin.

The next girl was tall with olive skin, deep blue eyes, and long dark brown hair.

"Ciao e benvenuto," she said in graceful Italian. "I'm Siena Moretti."

Phillips shook her hand and moved to the next boy, who was shorter than the rest by several inches but stood as straight and tall as his spiked-up black hair. "Niko Rodriguez," Phillips said. Niko didn't answer, only nodded and stepped back quickly.

His shyness stood in stark contrast to the next finalist in line—the blond girl in the wheelchair with sparkling blue eyes.

"Hello, Piper Williams," Phillips said. "Welcome."

"Thanks!" she replied brightly. "You didn't make a mistake."

"What do you mean?" Phillips asked.

Piper tapped the arm of her wheelchair and said, "This isn't a handicap."

"If I thought it was, you wouldn't be here."

"And thanks for the new wheels," she added. "They're pretty slick."

The wheelchair was a cross between a standard two-wheeled chair and a high-powered sport motorcycle.

"We felt you might need a little extra horsepower."

The smile dropped from Piper's face. "I don't need extra help."

"Glad to hear that, Piper," Phillips said.

Phillips moved on to the last candidate, a pale-skinned boy with an easy smile and relaxed stance.

"Dash Conroy," Phillips said, shaking his hand. "Welcome."

"Thanks," Dash replied with genuine enthusiasm. "This is pretty exciting."

Phillips gave him a conspiratorial wink and said, "You have no idea."

Phillips took a few steps back to address the entire group. "Welcome to you all. You know why you're here and how you came—"

"Where exactly are we?" Anna asked. "All I know is I was on a plane for hours, then driven through the desert. We could be in the middle of the Sahara."

"Not likely," Siena said. "Based on my flight time from Rome and seeing that Project Alpha is sponsored by the United States government, it's more likely we are in the continental United States."

Anna gave her a blank stare and said, "I wasn't serious about the Sahara."

"So then where are we?" Gabriel asked.

"I think we're at Area 51," Ravi announced. "I mean, we're talking about exploring outer space. What better place than where they keep all the aliens?"

"Sounds about right to me," Niko added. "That's in Nevada, right?"

"That is correct," Siena replied.

"You're hiding aliens here?" Anna asked Phillips. "Like, seriously?"

"Those are just rumors," Carly said. "There's never been proof and without proof they'll stay rumors."

"Do the winners get to see the aliens?" Ravi asked. "That would be cool."

"Yes!" Phillips blurted out, trying to contain his frustration.

The group stared at him in wonder.

Dash finally said, "Yes, there are aliens here?"

"No, there are no aliens here, but yes, this is Area 51."

"I knew it!" Ravi exclaimed, and held up his hand to Siena for a high five.

She didn't return it.

"If you would let me continue—" Phillips said patiently.

"Go ahead, chief," Ravi said. "This is your show."

"Thank you," Phillips said, taking a deep breath to regain his composure. "This base has been called Area 51, among many other names. For our mission, we are simply calling it Base Ten. I'm sorry to disappoint you but there are no aliens here."

Most of the kids shrugged and looked to the floor, disappointed.

"I knew that," Ravi said under his breath.

"For the next few weeks, you will be engaged in the final phase of the selection process. You know the purpose. With our natural fuel resources on the verge of depletion, the hunt for an alternate clean fuel source has been a primary goal of the US government and of many other countries around the world. Up to this point, those efforts have been unsuccessful, with one major exception."

"The Source," Dash said.

"Yes," Phillips replied. "The Source. Deep-space probes have located and identified a material we've been calling the Source on a celestial body far beyond our own solar system.

We believe the Source contains enough untapped energy that even a small amount will provide the power we so desperately need."

"What planet?" Anna asked. "Like . . . Pluto?"

"Pluto is no longer considered a planet," Siena said knowingly. "And it isn't outside our solar system."

"You know you're getting on my nerves, right?" Anna shot back.

"The exact location is also classified," Phillips said. "We've put a lot of resources into this mission; we don't need to be giving away our findings to competing outfits."

"So it's a race to get it first?" Niko asked.

"Not at all," Phillips replied. "The Source will benefit the entire planet."

"So then it shouldn't matter who gets it first, right?" Dash asked.

"It doesn't," Phillips said quickly, trying to avert another debate. "But this mission has been planned for many years. We know what we're doing and don't need outside interference."

"So what exactly is the mission?" Carly asked.

"Project Alpha will send a team of four into deep space to find the Source and bring it back to Earth. Simple as that. You're competing for the chance to be on the team that keeps Earth from going dark."

"And winning ten million dollars each," Anna said. "Don't forget that."

"And going down in history," Niko said. "That's okay too."

"Once the final four are selected," Phillips said, "there will be six months of training."

"You've really got a ship that can carry four of us into deep space?" Piper asked.

"Yeah," Gabriel added. "We don't even have a space shuttle anymore. How did we suddenly build a ship that can go all Star Wars?"

"I'll bet that's classified too," Niko said.

"It is," Phillips replied. "Not everything we develop makes it into the newspapers. But rest assured we can get you there. Our job now is to find the best kids for the job."

"Yeah, what's with that?" Anna asked. "Why kids?"

"It has to do with your metabolism," Phillips replied. "You asked if we had a ship to get you there. We do. But the technology is such that flying it would put too much strain on the systems of adults."

"But it's safe for kids?" Carly asked.

"It is."

"Promise?"

"There is no danger whatsoever," Phillips replied, trying to be patient.

"How will you choose who gets to go?" Piper asked.

"You will be put under the microscope. You'll be given tests. You will compete against each other and against yourselves. You're all brilliant kids. We know that. But we need to find the ones who can face the stress of the mission and still function at the highest levels."

"You mean you want to know who's going to crack," Anna said.

"That's one way of putting it," Phillips replied. "There's one mantra we live by: failure is not an option."

"What kind of tests?" Piper asked.

"Contests. Competitions. Puzzles. We're going to expose you to many different types of situations. It isn't just about who performs the best; it's about which four will combine to make the best team."

"When do we start?" Dash asked.

"Right now," Phillips replied with a smile.

3

"**The first competition** is about how you want to spend your time here. You will be living in dorms. Boys in one, girls in the other. They are functional and comfortable."

"Kind of like camp," Niko said.

"However," Phillips continued, "one of you will be invited to stay in your own private quarters with a queen bed, a private bathroom, and your own refrigerator."

"Who gets to stay there?" Carly asked.

Phillips held up a handkerchief-sized golden flag.

"Your first challenge," he declared. "Scattered throughout the arena are a few dozen golden flags like this one. Some are in plain sight, others you'll have to hunt for. The first person who retrieves four flags will be staying in the superior quarters for the duration of your stay. Question is, how badly do you want it?"

The kids all stood staring at Phillips, not sure how to react.

Phillips pointed to a door on the far side of the hangar and said, "The arena is through there. The competition begins . . . now."

Anna took off running. Niko was right behind her. The others followed quickly.

The final phase of the Project Alpha competition was under way.

It began as a frantic free-for-all, like a massive Easter egg hunt with a lot more at stake than snapping up a few chocolate eggs. Anna sprinted across the empty hangar and spotted the first flag hanging next to the door leading to the arena. She snatched it off the hook and held it up in triumph.

"That room is mine!" she declared, then waved to the others and ran out the door.

Gabriel, Niko, Ravi, and Siena sprinted for the door and blasted through right behind her.

Dash took his time. He did a quick scan of the entire space, checking for more flags. There were none, so he ran for the door but stopped when he saw that stacked next to it was an odd assortment of equipment. There were several coils of red climbing rope, a pile of fleecy pullovers of various bright colors, and four ice axes hanging from hooks.

"Strange equipment to be in an airplane hangar," Carly said as she jogged up from behind him.

"Maybe there's a flag buried in there," Dash said, and quickly dug through the jackets.

"Too obvious," Piper said as she flew by them.

She spun the wheelchair around expertly and backed into the door, pushing it open. She rolled outside but held it for the other two.

"Coming?" she called.

Dash and Carly gave each other quick looks and ran outside.

The air temperature had plummeted to below freezing.

"This is impossible," Carly said. "We're in the desert."

"Cool," Piper said with wonder. "Literally."

"That answers one thing," Dash said. He ran back inside and moments later came back with three jackets, a coil of rope, and three ice axes. "This stuff is here for a reason," he said as he handed jackets and axes to Piper and Carly.

The three slipped on the jackets, then scanned the area to see nothing but dense fog.

"What's this about?" Piper asked in a low voice as if not wanting to be heard by anyone other than Dash and Carly.

"Our first test," Carly said. "I'll bet there's a whole lot more going on here than a race for a couple of flags."

The three moved forward cautiously, straining to see through the heavy mist. None said it out loud, but they felt safer together than going at it alone.

"I see one!" Piper exclaimed. She shot forward to where a golden flag hung from a three-foot-high pole. She grabbed it, spun back to the others, and held it up, saying, "The sooner one of us gets four, the sooner we can get out of this freezer."

A hulking shadow moved through the mist behind Piper. Only Dash and Carly saw it. It was a fleeting glimpse but it was real. And it was big.

"What was that?" Dash exclaimed.

Piper spun around but saw nothing. "What was what?" she asked.

"I saw it too," Carly answered. "It looked like a big guy, moving fast."

"Anna?" Dash called out.

"I got another one!" Anna called from somewhere in the distance.

"I don't like this contest," Carly said nervously.

"Maybe that's the point," Dash said. "They're testing our nerves."

"I'm freezing," Piper said, her teeth chattering.

"Then let's move," Dash said, and they continued on.

They walked cautiously but after taking only a few steps, Carly slipped and had to fight to keep her balance.

"Whoa! Ice!" she cried as her feet slid out, and she hit the ground hard. "Ow. That is just rude."

Dash helped her to her feet. "It's an ice rink," he said. "Don't walk; slide."

"Look!" Piper exclaimed, pointing.

Another big shadow shot through the distant mist.

"That's not Anna," Piper said, her voice cracking. "It looks like a Sasquatch. Or a Wookiee."

"There's something over there," Dash said, moving ahead.

The three cautiously slid forward until a massive white mound appeared out of the mist.

"It's a pile of snow," Carly said. "Or a monster igloo."

"There's a cave," Dash said.

A jagged opening was cut in the face of the huge frozen mound.

"Did the shadow thing go in there?" Piper asked nervously.

"We should go see," Dash said. "I guarantee it's part of the game."

"I can't," Piper said. "I won't be able to turn the chair around in there."

"I'll go," Carly said.

"We'll go together," Dash said, and the two of them slipped through the opening.

"Cool," Piper said. "Be careful."

It was dark inside, but the ice gave off a faint glow that was enough for them to see by.

"It's an ice tunnel," Carly said. "There's gotta be a flag in here somewhere."

The tunnel twisted sharply, creating blind turns with no way of knowing what might be lurking around the next corner. Dash and Carly walked shoulder to shoulder until . . .

CRACK.

The sound came from beyond the next sharp turn.

They froze.

"Something's in there," Carly whispered.

Dash fought the urge to turn and run. Instead, he steeled himself and yelled a warning. "There are two of us!"

He lifted the ice ax and held it out threateningly, though his hands were shaking.

CRACK!

Whatever was making the sound was moving closer.

It was too late to turn and run. Carly and Dash pushed closer to one another and tensed up.

CRACK!

A footstep crunched the ice just beyond the turn.

Dash raised the ice ax . . .

. . . as a hand appeared from around the corner, waving a golden flag.

"I'm afraid you are too late," said a girl as she stepped around the corner.

"Siena," Dash said with a relieved gasp.

Carly could breathe again.

"There is a cavern at the end of the tunnel but there was only one flag," Siena said. "Check for yourself but it would be a waste of time because if there was more than one, I would have taken it."

"Did you see a big guy lurking around?" Carly asked.

"No, but nothing would surprise me. This is quite the elaborate challenge. My guess is they erected a climate-controlled enclosure to house this frigid environment. Now if you will excuse me"—she pushed past the others, headed for the mouth of the cave—"I have two more flags to find."

"You already found two?" Carly asked.

Siena held up two flags as she disappeared around the icy bend.

"Is it me or does she sound like a computer?" Carly whispered.

Dash laughed and said, "Let's get out of here."

They walked quickly back the way they had come and made it to the mouth of the cave with minimal slippage.

Piper was waiting for them with a big smile. "Look," she said, pointing higher up on the icy mound.

Dash and Carly turned to see three golden flags on a ledge, thirty feet up.

"I didn't tell Siena," Piper said with an innocent smile.

"So close," Dash said. "But there's no way to get them."

Carly held up her ice ax. "No?"

The shaft was metallic silver with a black rubber hand grip on one end and a nasty-looking point on the other.

"They're climbing tools," he said.

"You need two to climb, which means we both can't do it," Carly said.

Dash looked up to the flags. He'd never used ice axes before.

"I'll try," Dash said. "If I get 'em, we'll each take a flag."

"You'd do that?" Piper asked.

"Sure. You found 'em, Carly's giving up her ax, and I'm climbing. That's fair."

Carly handed over her ax and said, "Be careful."

Dash grasped both axes, wrapped the safety straps around his wrists, and faced the icy surface.

"How hard could it be, right?" he asked, not sounding very confident.

He raised the ax in his right hand and hammered it against the ice. It caught and stuck firmly. He did the same with his left hand, a little bit higher. With his foot on the surface, he pulled himself off the ground. The surface sloped away from him at enough of an angle that it wasn't a difficult climb.

"It's easy," Dash said. "If it were any steeper I'd be in trouble."

At that exact moment, his sneaker slipped off and his stomach smashed against the ice.

"Ouch."

"You sure about that?" Carly asked.

His answer was to find a better toe hold and then yank the right ax out of the ice. He reached up as high as he could and hammered it home again.

"I got this," Dash said.

Looking up, he saw that the ledge was right below the top of the frozen mound. It only took another minute and three more whacks at the ice to reach it. He hoisted himself up, stood on the ledge so that his head cleared the top of the mound . . .

. . . and came face to face with a weird white beast that was climbing up the other side. Its fiery red eyes glowed from deep sockets in a massive head.

"Ahhh!" Dash screamed, and pushed away from the beast.

He fell backward on the ledge but had the presence of mind to reach out with one of the axes to grab at the ice. It stopped him from sliding all the way to the ground but he hung there by one hand. With a surge of adrenaline, Dash slammed the other ax into the ice. He shifted his weight and repeated the process until he finished a controlled slide back to the ground.

"What happened?" Piper asked anxiously.

"I saw what was making the shadow," Dash said, breathing hard. "It was a . . . a . . . monster. A big white monster thing. I fell back and . . . I didn't get the flags. Sorry."

"This is getting too crazy," Carly said. "Maybe we should just hang together and—"

"Help!" came someone's scream from somewhere off in the fog.

"Oh man, now what?" Piper said.

"Help me!" the desperate voice called out again.

"C'mon!" Dash said, and moved quickly into the fog, headed in the direction of the sound. Between zero visibility and the icy surface, it was slow going.

"I've got traction," Piper said, and zoomed ahead.

They soon heard the sound of splashing, thrashing water.

"I can't breathe," the voice yelled.

"Be careful," Carly said to Piper. "You're headed toward—"

Dash leapt forward and grabbed the back of Piper's wheelchair, stopping her from rolling off the edge of the ice and into a frothing pool.

"—water."

"Oops," Piper said, breathless. "Thanks."

"Who's out there?" Carly called.

"It's Niko!" came the desperate shout. "The ice broke and . . . and . . . it's so cold I can't catch my breath!"

"Here," Carly said, grabbing the rope and uncoiling it.

"We're throwing you a lifeline," Dash yelled.

"Hurry!" Niko pleaded.

"Tie the end to your chair," Dash said to Piper.

While Piper looped the end around the arm of her wheelchair, Dash took the rest of the rope and slid closer to the edge.

"Where are you?" he called out.

"Here!" Niko responded.

The fog was so dense, Dash couldn't see him.

"Ready!" Piper called out.

"Here it comes!" Dash hurled the rope in the direction of Niko's voice. There was a splash and then . . .

"I got it!" Niko cried with relief.

"Hang on, we'll pull you out!" Dash yelled.

He immediately started pulling but the surface was too slippery and his feet went out from under him. He sat down and tried yanking the rope again but only ended up pulling himself closer to the edge.

"I can't get traction," he called to the others with growing panic.

"I can," Piper said. "Let it go."

Dash released the rope and Piper pulled it all the way in.

"I can't hold on!" Niko called.

"Help me," Piper shouted to Carly. "Stand on the back and hang on to the rope."

Carly grabbed the rope with one hand and stood on the back of the chair. Piper took hold of the controls. She jammed the vehicle into reverse and eased open the throttle. Slowly, the chair moved backward.

"Hang on, Niko!" Dash yelled.

The wheels dug into the ice and kept moving as they gradually pulled Niko closer.

"There he is!" Dash called out.

The four other candidates skidded up out of the fog, watching in wonder as Niko was towed to the edge of the ice. Dash grabbed him and pulled him up onto the slick surface. Niko was breathing hard and shivering.

Piper pulled off her jacket and threw it to Dash.

"Wrap him up," she commanded. "If we don't get his body temperature up, it could hurt his heart."

Dash pulled off his own jacket as well and put both jackets on Niko.

"Rub his back to get his blood moving faster," Piper added.

Dash followed orders and rubbed Niko's back.

"I'm okay," Niko said through chattering teeth. "Thanks."

Piper and Carly exchanged high fives.

"I saw a flag and went for it," Niko said. "But the ice gave way."

"Did you get the flag?" Anna asked.

Niko shook his head.

"Well, I got three," Anna announced. "The game's still on."

"No, it isn't," Piper announced, and handed her flag to Anna.

"Seriously?" Anna said with surprise.

"Congratulations."

A loud horn sounded as bright lights kicked on, bathing the group in warm white light. The whirring sound of giant fans filled the arena as the fog was blown away. Within seconds, the entire area was revealed.

"Exactly as I suspected," Siena said with a smug smile.

They were in a giant white tent that was large enough to house a twelve-ring circus. Ice covered the entire floor like a giant hockey rink. Five different ice mounds like the one Dash had climbed were scattered about. The water that Niko had fallen into was a moat that surrounded an island with the largest mound.

A metal catwalk ringed the tent high above them. Hanging below it were multiple high-intensity lights. The air temperature rose quickly to a more desertlike norm.

"Well done!" Commander Phillips exclaimed as he strode toward them. "We have a winner of the Tundra Event."

Anna held up the four flags triumphantly.

"What is this place?" Gabriel asked. "It's like some funhouse arctic weirdness."

"This is the arena where many of your challenges will take place," Phillips replied. "In here, we can create any kind of environment and situation. Niko, you were never in danger."

He pointed to the moat where several frogmen had surfaced and gave a thumbs-up.

"I just hope I don't die of pneumonia," Niko replied.

"What about the monster?" Dash asked. "What was that about?"

"Just another element of surprise," Phillips explained. "We need to see how each of you will react under different forms of stress."

"How did we do?" Carly asked.

Phillips smiled and said, "That's for me to discuss with the rest of the Project Alpha team. Now, everyone back into the hangar where you'll be taken to your quarters. It's been a long day. Anna, you'll be shown to your private room."

"Yes!" Anna exclaimed, and hurried off.

Phillips stepped up to Niko and helped him to his feet.

"How do you feel?" Phillips asked.

"Cold and wet," Niko replied. "But ready for the next contest."

"That's what I like to hear. Go get dried off."

Niko headed for the hangar, followed by Siena, Ravi, and Gabriel.

Dash stood up and went to Carly and Piper. The three exchanged high fives.

"Not bad," Dash said.

"Tell me," Phillips said to Piper, "why did you give up your flag?"

"I wanted the contest to be over," she said. "Besides, I didn't want the prize."

"You didn't want a private room?" Phillips asked, surprised.

"Nope," Piper said. "I didn't come here to be alone."

"I see," Phillips said with no emotion. "Go join the others."

The three headed off, leaving Phillips in the middle of the arena. He surveyed the scene with satisfaction as the ice melted around him.

He then looked up to the catwalk.

Looking down was a single observer wearing a blue jumpsuit similar to the one Phillips wore. It was a teenager with short blond hair who stood leaning on the guardrail. At his feet sat a golden retriever.

"Thoughts?" Phillips called up.

"Eight solid candidates," the young man called back. "Let's hope they can handle it when things really get rough."

4

Four hundred miles to the southwest of Base Ten, a small group of men and women sat huddled over consoles in a high-tech control room that was buried deep within the Sierra Nevada Mountains. Twenty different computer monitors covered the front wall, each showing a different live view of Base Ten.

The large monitor in the center showed footage of the Project Alpha candidates working through the Tundra Event. Dash climbed the ice mound; Niko fell through the ice; Piper and Carly pulled him out using the rope and the wheelchair; Anna raised the golden flags triumphantly.

In the center of the room, intently scrutinizing the action, was a man standing ramrod-straight. He had a shock of silver-gray hair and intense dark eyes that didn't miss a single detail.

"We've downloaded all footage from the event, sir," announced a young woman who sat at one console.

"Understood," the man replied. "Continue uploading the feed from the arena until it goes dark."

"Yes sir," the woman replied with a hint of concern. She turned around. "But is that—?" She stopped herself.

The gray-haired man tore his gaze from the monitor and shot a look at her.

"Is that what?" he asked curtly.

The other technicians kept their eyes on their monitors. They didn't want any part of this conversation.

"Nothing, sir," the woman said quickly. She turned back to her monitor.

"Is that what?" the man repeated impatiently.

The woman didn't want to answer but had no choice.

"Is that pushing our luck?" she finally blurted out. "The more time we're tied into their system, the more chance there is of being discovered."

The woman felt the heat of his steady glare on the back of her head.

"O'Mara!" the man yelled abruptly, startling everyone.

"Yes sir," another technician, O'Mara, replied obediently.

"Relieve her," the man said, and turned his attention back to the center monitor.

The woman stared at the man, her mouth open in shock.

"But it was just a question," she said.

"You have doubts," the man said without looking at her. "I have no patience for doubt."

She couldn't find the words to argue, so she stood and left the control room quickly with her head down while O'Mara took her place.

"Upload continuing," he declared. "We're still tied into Base Ten."

“Thank you,” the man said. “It’s a joy to see all the hard work they’re doing . . . to ensure the success of *our* mission.”

The man turned on his heel and strode for the door.

“Alert me the moment they begin the next challenge,” he declared as he left the control room.

When the door closed behind him, every last person in the room breathed a deep sigh of relief.

5

The eight candidates were brought to the dormitory building by a military aide who showed them the girls' dorm on the ground floor and the boys' on the second. Anna's private room was on the third floor.

"Penthouse, baby!" Anna said as she left the others with a quick wave.

"Nice work today, guys," the military aide told them. "Welcome aboard."

With quick good-byes, the boys and girls separated and went to the rooms that would be their homes during the competition.

The boys' dorm was one large room with two bunk beds along opposite walls. There were four desks with chairs and a laptop on each. On the beds were their backpacks. They were allowed to bring items from home, but told not to bring clothes because they would be given uniforms. As promised, the uniforms were laid out next to the backpacks. Each bunk held a pair of light gray running pants along with a long-sleeved workout top. The right half and sleeve were navy blue; the left was brilliant orange. There were also low black cross-trainers, orange socks, and orange boxer shorts.

Ravi picked up the shirt and said, "Are we going to space or the circus?"

"I need to meditate," Niko said.

"Uh, what?" Gabriel asked.

Niko climbed up onto an upper bunk and sat cross-legged in the center. He closed his eyes, rested his hands on his knees, and took several slow deep breaths.

The other three boys exchanged confused looks.

"Don't look at me like that," Niko said without opening his eyes. "I just had a near-death experience and my core body temperature dropped. I need to get realigned."

"Or you could just take a hot shower," Ravi said.

"Meditation taps into the deeper powers of the mind to heal the body," Niko said. "You would be amazed at what the power of proper meditation can do."

"If it's that powerful," Ravi said, "meditate me up a spot in the final four."

Niko ignored him and slipped deeper into his meditative state. Ravi looked at the others and spun his finger next to his head in the universal "crazy" gesture.

Dash and Gabriel took the other bunk beds. Dash below, Gabriel above. They both went right to their packs and began emptying them.

"Where are you from?" Dash asked.

"Outside Chicago. We got a big old house for a big old family. Two sisters and two brothers. I'm square in the middle. Add in my parents and grandparents and it gets pretty crazy. What about you?"

"It's just my mom and little sister. We live in Orlando."

"Really? You got Mickey Mouse for a neighbor?"

"Yeah," Dash said with a laugh. "We hang out all the time."

Gabriel laughed too. "Hey, if I lived there, I'd be going to Disney World every day."

Dash shrugged. "That would get expensive."

"Ten million bucks would fix that real quick," Gabriel said.

Gabriel pulled a few items from his pack: a small tool kit, books, and a stuffed koala bear that he quickly hid under his pillow.

"Is that why you're doing this?" Dash asked. "The money?"

"Absolutely," Gabriel replied. "That kind of cash could set up my family forever."

"And solve the world's energy crises," Dash added as he climbed up onto his bunk.

"Yeah, that too. I wouldn't mind being a hero. What about you? Don't you care about the money?"

"Well, sure," Dash said. "It would be great if Mom didn't have to worry about money anymore, but mostly I'm doing it because I'm scared."

"What?" Gabriel exclaimed.

Ravi had been listening and leaned a little closer.

Niko opened one eye.

"If you're scared, you are in the wrong place," Gabriel said.

Dash took out a framed photo of himself, his mom, and his little sister. All three wore big, happy smiles. He gently placed it on a shelf above his bed.

"I'm not scared about the mission," Dash said. "What scares me is a world without power. Money won't matter much if we all get sent back to the Stone Age."

Gabriel had no comeback.

"I say we make a pact," Ravi said, jumping out of his bunk. "The four of us guys should be the ones to go on this mission. We don't need girls out there. Especially that Anna. She's wound a little too tight. We gotta do everything we can to make sure we're the final four. What d'ya say?"

Dash and Gabriel hesitated, not sure how to answer. Dash opened his mouth to speak and . . .

"Excellent! You are making yourself at home!" came a tinny, cheerful boy's voice through a speaker.

Everyone looked around for the speaker, but instead saw a visitor.

It wasn't a boy.

It was a robot.

"Well, this is different," Gabriel said, stunned.

The robot stood three feet tall and had two arms, two legs, and a wide head with two lenses that looked like eyes. Its plastic-cased body was mostly white, while all the joints were a mix of black and metal, lit up by glowing blue lights that emanated from within. Its tiny hands were fully functional, complete with opposable thumbs. And though it had rather substantial feet, it almost seemed to glide like a hovercraft when it moved from place to place. It walked toward the boys with a fluid motion. There was nothing robotic or stilted about its movement.

"Welcome to you," the robot said warmly. "I am STEAM 6000. Call me STEAM. Yes sir!"

Niko and Dash climbed down from their bunks. None of them could take their eyes off the little machine.

"You're a—you're a . . . robot," Niko said numbly.

"He probably knows that," Ravi said.

"Maybe it's a she," Dash said.

"I am neither," STEAM said. "Shawn gave me a boy voice, so you might as well refer to me as 'he.' "

"Shawn?" Niko asked.

"Commander Phillips," STEAM replied.

"He made you?" Dash asked.

"Yes sir," STEAM replied. "I will assist you through the selection process and training. I will try to answer your questions and help make the experience as easy as possible."

The four boys stared at the little robot in wonder.

"Man, this day just keeps on getting stranger," Ravi said.

STEAM walked back for the door. "Put on your uniforms and meet outside. Time for dinner. I will alert the girls."

STEAM pushed open the door and left.

The four guys stood there with their mouths hanging open.

Finally Ravi called out, "Okay, bye!"

"That really happened, right?" Niko said, dumbfounded.

"Who is this Phillips guy?" Gabriel asked. "He's running this whole show and still has time to invent talking robots?"

"He must be a genius," Niko replied. "It's not going to be easy to impress somebody like that."

The four boys looked at one another, remembering that they were in a competition.

"Remember," Ravi said. "The guys gotta stick together. Everything we do has to be about bouncing the girls. Just keep it on the down low. Right?"

"Let's go eat," Dash said, ducking the question.

The boys got changed and walked down the stairs that led

to the first-floor common area. Waiting for them were Siena, Carly, and Piper. All three were dressed in their orange-and-blue uniforms.

"Look at us!" Ravi announced. "If we don't make the team, we can always get jobs at Jiffy Burger."

"I think they're cool," Piper said.

An elevator door slid open to reveal Anna and STEAM.

Anna hurried out of the elevator, looking irritated.

"Back off!" she shouted, pointing a finger at the robot.

She went right up to the others and stood behind Piper's wheelchair for protection.

"What's the matter?" Piper asked.

"That talking Lego is freaking me out," Anna said, clearly upset. "I didn't bust my butt to get here just to have some plastic WALL-E Pillow Pet telling me what to do."

"I do not mean to upset you, Anna," STEAM said. "I want to make things as easy as possible for you. Yes sir!"

"Yeah, well, no sir!" Anna shot back. "If you really want to make it easier on me, waddle yourself on out of here."

"I will do my best to stay out of your way," STEAM said. "Everyone please follow me to the dining hall."

STEAM hurried out of the building with quick short strides. Everyone followed except Anna. Dash saw that she wasn't coming and went back to her.

"You okay?" he asked.

"I'm fine," she said sharply. "I just didn't expect to have some mechanical Munchkin knocking on my door."

"It kind of threw me too. Maybe you should sleep in the dorm with the other girls. Being alone is only gonna make it tougher to—"

"Whoa, stop," Anna barked. "I earned that room and you want me to give it up?"

"No! We're all in this together and I thought it might be easier—"

"We are not in this together," Anna snapped. "When the final four get picked, I'll care about the other three but until then we are in an eight-way fight. So back off."

Anna stormed off after the others, leaving Dash with his mouth hanging open.

Up until that moment, he had only thought of the competition as being about proving himself. It was him against the various tests and challenges. He hadn't thought much about having to compete against others. Now, between Ravi trying to create a secret alliance and Anna throwing down the gauntlet, he was faced with another reality. He not only had to prove himself, he had to worry about seven others who were in a desperate fight to win.

And he had only been there for three hours.

6

"I love this place!" Ravi exclaimed as he went back for his third piece of key lime pie.

The meal was extraordinary, with every candidate getting plenty of their favorite food. There was pizza, BBQ, roast turkey, burgers, hot dogs, and even spicy chicken fingers. Five different kinds of salads were available along with baked, mashed, French fried, and sweet potatoes. They even served plantains, cheese fondue, and sushi. The desserts were impossibly good with cakes, pies, eight different flavors of ice cream, and heaping bowls of fresh fruit.

The chefs had outdone themselves because they knew what everyone loved based on their profiles. The kids ate by themselves in a small dining room. Nobody talked much. It had been a long, tiring day and this feast was exactly what they needed.

Finally, after an hour of feasting, the last dirty fork clattered down.

"Who wants seconds?" STEAM announced as he strode into the room.

He was met with a chorus of groans.

STEAM said, "It is good you enjoyed the food. It was a special meal to make you feel at home."

"Home?" Gabriel called out. "I don't eat like this at home."

"So what's next, little guy?" Ravi asked.

"Bedtime," STEAM said. "Tomorrow the competition continues."

"Bed?" Anna exclaimed. "It's only like . . . nine o'clock."

"Twenty fifty-nine," STEAM countered. "The evening meal will not always go this late. Lights go out at twenty-one hundred hours."

"Why so strict on the time?" Dash asked.

Suddenly, the room turned dead-black. Everyone fell silent.

"Whoa," Carly said. "You weren't kidding about lights-out."

"It is the blackout," STEAM said. "Every night. Power will return at zero five hundred tomorrow."

It was a sober reminder as to why they were there. Yes, they were vying to take part in the adventure of a lifetime and a ten-million-dollar prize, but the purpose was to save the world from going dark. Forever.

"Wow," Dash said. "Even the government gets blacked out."

"How do we get back?" Piper asked nervously. "I can't see a thing."

Two beams of light shot from STEAM's "eyes." "I will guide you, yes sir!"

STEAM walked for the door. Everyone scrambled to get up and follow while trying not to trip over their chairs. Soon they were walking two by two across the quiet sandy road that cut through the desert base.

Night had come to the desert. Not a single light shone from the buildings, but the sky was alive with the twinkling lights from an uncountable number of stars.

Dash stopped and stared up at the brilliant umbrella.

"I wonder which one we're going to?" he asked nobody in particular.

Piper stopped next to him and looked skyward.

"I try not to think about it," she said. "I don't want to get my hopes up and then be disappointed if I don't make the team."

"Too late for me," Dash said. "I want this really bad."

"Me too," Piper said. "I know I'm good enough; I just hope Commander Phillips thinks so."

"I wouldn't stress if I were you," Dash said. "The way you saved Niko today? That was awesome."

"It was a team effort," Piper said with a humble shrug.

"I guess," Dash said. "If you ever want to team up again, let me know."

Piper smiled and said, "Same here."

She held out her hand to shake and Dash took it.

"Hey!" Gabriel called. "Catch up!"

The two took off, hurrying after the others.

Dash was happy to have made a friend in Piper, but as they approached the group, he realized his dilemma had just deepened. Ravi was expecting him to be in an alliance of boys, yet he had just made an agreement to team up with a girl. Either way, somebody was going to be angry with him. Dash couldn't be sure if he was making friends or lining up enemies.

Fifteen minutes later, everyone was in their bunks, ready for sleep.

"Power is back at zero five hundred," STEAM announced

to the boys. "Be showered, dressed, and ready for breakfast by zero six hundred. Understood?"

All the guys grunted an exhausted "yes."

"Perfect," STEAM said. "I am going to make like a tree and get out of here. Good night."

With that, the little robot left and closed the door.

"What did he say?" Gabriel asked. "That made no sense."

"Maybe the blackout scrambled his circuits," Ravi said.

"I don't think I can sleep," Niko said.

They were the last words anybody heard before they all fell asleep.

The only one who didn't nod off was Gabriel. He lay in his bunk with his eyes wide open. The wheels in his mechanically adept brain were grinding away. Something didn't feel right to him. Gabriel prided himself on being able to figure out how things worked, whether it was a complex machine or a string of computer code. He could see twenty moves ahead in a chess game and predict the exact outcome or listen to a car engine and know which cylinder was sticking.

He didn't know exactly what was bothering him except that something felt off. He also knew that his brain wouldn't let him sleep until he figured out what it was. He had no choice but to get up and go for a walk. Carefully, quietly, he slipped out of his bunk, put on his uniform, and tiptoed for the door. With one last look to make sure he hadn't disturbed the others, he left the boys' dorm.

His plan was to go outside, take a few laps around the building to clear his head, and then try to sleep. The plan changed when he got halfway down the stairs to the lobby and saw the shadow of someone sitting on the bottom step. He froze.

"I heard you," a voice said from the step.

Busted. Gabriel gave up trying to be sneaky and walked down the stairs.

Sitting at the bottom, still dressed in her uniform, was Carly.

"You can't sleep either?" Gabriel asked.

"How can anybody sleep knowing what we're going to face tomorrow?" she asked.

"We'll do fine," Gabriel said. "We wouldn't be here if they didn't think we could handle it."

"I know," Carly said. "But what's getting to me is the unknown. What kind of tests are they going to give us? That freezing-fog thing was crazy."

"I know, right?" Gabriel said with a laugh. "Abominable snow dude? Didn't see that one coming."

"Exactly!" Carly exclaimed. "These aren't tests you can study for. I'm a studier. I like to be prepared."

"I think that's the point. They want to see how we'll do when we don't see what's coming."

Carly nodded thoughtfully. "I guess, but that's not how I operate."

"Don't tell anybody," Gabriel said. "If they think you're nervous, they'll be all over you like sharks in bloody water. There's already a plan to—"

Gabriel stopped talking. He had said too much.

"Plan to what?" Carly asked.

Gabriel thought fast but couldn't come up with anything.

"All right," he said. "Some of the guys are talking about working together to make sure we win."

"You mean to make sure the girls lose," Carly said.

"I didn't buy it," Gabriel said quickly. "I don't think Dash did either. But it was Ravi's idea and Niko is probably meditating about it right now."

"Meditating?"

"Don't ask. Just watch your back, okay?"

Carly gave Gabriel a smile and said, "Thanks. Why can't *you* sleep?"

Gabriel's eyes narrowed down. That's what he did when he was working on a problem.

"It's this blackout. We're on a military base. They wouldn't black out an entire military base. Especially not one that's trying to solve the world's energy problem."

"Maybe they don't have a choice," Carly offered. "We really are running out of energy."

"Maybe," Gabriel said, still squinting. "But there's something else. I can hear it. This base isn't dead. Something's got power."

"You can hear that?" Carly asked.

Gabriel shrugged. "What can I say? I'm fine-tuned."

Carly thought for a second, then stood up.

"So let's go find it," she declared.

"Wait, what?" Gabriel asked nervously. "We can't go poking around this place."

"Why not? Now you've got me interested." She walked for the door, turned back to Gabriel, and said, "Coming?"

Gabriel hesitated. As curious as he was, he didn't want to do anything that would hurt his chances of making the team.

But his curiosity won. It always did.

When they stepped outside of the dorm, Gabriel stood still and listened.

Carly listened too. "All I hear is the wind—"

"Shh!" he said, holding up his hand. "There's a steady hum. The frequency means it's definitely man-made."

He walked off quickly, following his ears and his instinct. Carly was right on his heels. They moved through the dark base, hugging the buildings for fear of getting caught. There weren't many people around. They passed a few soldiers who hurried along with their heads down but that was it.

Suddenly, Gabriel grabbed Carly and pulled her into a doorway.

"What's wrong?" she asked nervously.

A second later, a jeep flew by without its headlights on.

"I heard that coming a while ago," Gabriel said.

"Wow, you're like a cat."

Gabriel walked quickly, like a bloodhound closing on its quarry. Carly had to jog to keep pace. They rounded the corner of a hangar and found themselves in front of a vast one-story building that looked large enough to encompass an entire city block.

"Whatever the sound is, it's coming from in there," Gabriel said. "Still want to see?"

Carly nodded enthusiastically.

They jogged across the road and up to a door. Gabriel grabbed the handle, hesitated a moment for fear it would be locked, and pulled.

It opened.

"I can feel the vibration through my feet," Gabriel said.

"You're kind of odd, you know that?" Carly said.

They entered a long, dark corridor. Gabriel put his hand on the wall, feeling the vibration. Slowly, he walked to his right while running his hand along the wall.

"It's getting more intense," he said.

They continued for several yards until they came upon a door on the inside wall.

Carly put her hand on it.

"Whatever it is, it's stronger in there," she said.

A ribbon of light shone from beneath the door.

"Either they're burning torches in there, or they've got power," Gabriel said.

He grabbed the door handle, pressed it down, and pushed the door open.

The steady hum they had been following grew louder. Cautiously, they poked their heads through the doorway.

"Oh man," Gabriel said.

Carly's eyes went wide. "What is this?"

"Some kind of control room," Gabriel said in awe.

On the far side of the large room was a series of touch-screen monitors on a long counter. All showed rapidly changing data. Beyond the monitors, separated by a glass wall, were three giant steel-encased devices. They were lying side by side, each the size of an eighteen-wheeler truck.

Carly and Gabriel drifted closer.

"They're turbines," Gabriel answered with authority.

"So they're generating power after all," Carly said.

On the far side of the room, a door opened.

Carly and Gabriel quickly hid behind a bank of hard drives.

Two women in blue coveralls came in and stood at the control board to read the monitors.

"Let's keep number two online at fifty percent," one woman said. "Bring one and three down to five percent. We'll bring them both back up at four forty-five tomorrow."

“Yes, ma’am,” the second woman said.

The first woman left and the second ran her fingers over the center console, sliding down two of the controls. Instantly, the tone of the generators changed as two of the machines powered down. Satisfied that all was well, she left the way she came in.

Carly gestured to Gabriel to head out and hurried for the door.

Gabriel didn’t follow. He drifted back to the control board as if drawn by a magnetic force. He focused on the controls of the touch screen, his eyes narrowing.

“What are you doing?” Carly whispered nervously as she rejoined him.

“The base is totally shut down,” Gabriel said, thinking out loud. “What are they using this power for?”

The door on the far side of the room began to open again.

Carly grabbed Gabriel and pulled him toward the exit.

The two retraced their steps without a word and hurried back to the dorm. Once inside, they finally relaxed. Both were breathing hard from the run.

“Why would they say there’s a blackout when they have plenty of power?” Carly asked.

“I don’t know,” Gabriel replied. “But it means they’re not being totally honest with us. I don’t like that. We should tell the others.”

Carly thought hard, then said, “Are you sure about that? We might be making a big deal out of nothing. I’d wait until we know more.”

Gabriel took a deep breath to calm down. He looked square into Carly’s eyes as if trying to read her.

"All right, I won't tell anybody," Gabriel said. "But I don't like secrets and I don't like feeling like I'm on my own here."

"You're not on your own—you've got me," Carly said. "I owe you for telling me about Ravi's plan. Good night."

She spun on her heel and walked toward the girls' dorm. She stopped and turned back to Gabriel with a smile.

"Thanks, that was fun," she said. Then she disappeared down the hall.

Gabriel watched her for a moment, then said to himself, "Fun?" He thought about it and smiled. "Yeah, I guess it was."

He ran up the stairs taking two at a time.

7

"I hope you all had a good night's rest," Commander Phillips said as he strode into the hangar where the kids had first met him.

Carly threw Gabriel a sly smile.

STEAM had brought all eight candidates to the hangar, where they found three car-sized clear plastic spheres suspended inside large metal frames. Inside each sphere was a high-tech cockpit. One side of each sphere was open, allowing access.

"These are flight simulators," Phillips explained. "The controls match those that you'll use on your journey."

Phillips reached inside one of the simulators and retrieved a sleek pair of sunglasses.

"Your ship will be programmed to get you to your destination, but there may come a time that it will need to be flown manually."

"Whoa, is anybody here a pilot?" Niko asked.

"Not yet," Phillips said as he put on the glasses. "The controls are intuitive. They read your eye movement and thought patterns. Basically, you think about what you want to do and the ship will respond accordingly."

“That seems impossible,” Siena said skeptically.

“It does, but it isn’t,” Phillips said. “Our goal here is to see which of you is most capable of flying. Who wants to try first?”

Anna jumped to the front. Ravi’s hand shot up as did Gabriel’s.

“Okay, then,” Phillips said. “Let’s go for a ride.”

All three strapped into the cushioned flight seats and put on the glasses.

Phillips said, “Now place your hand on the glass pad to your right. The controls respond to hand pressure. It’s the third input source that determines your course.”

When they put their hands on their pads, a monitor in front of each came to life that showed a star field.

“Now fly,” Phillips instructed. “Maneuver the ship through the markers.”

Scattered across the star field were dozens of colorful orbs that created a virtual obstacle course.

“This is awesome!” Gabriel exclaimed as his “ship” traveled the course.

As they moved, the cockpit moved with them, giving them the sensation of flight. It even shuddered when an orb was hit. In minutes, they all got the hang of it and were speeding through the maze. Dash, Siena, and Carly went next, followed by Niko and Piper.

“It’s simple,” Ravi boasted. “Like flying an Xbox.”

After an hour of practice, Phillips gathered them together.

“Who feels confident?” he asked.

Everyone raised their hand.

“All right, then. Let’s find out who the real pilots are.”

The kids tensed up. This was it. Their next competition.

"We'll start with Carly, Niko, and Siena. This is an individual challenge. You're all going to fly through the exact same simulated asteroid field as if you were traveling side by side. The winner will be the one who makes it through the fastest with the least amount of damage."

"Let's do it!" Niko exclaimed.

The three strapped into the simulators.

"C'mon, Niko!" Ravi exclaimed. "Show the girls how it's done!"

Carly looked at Gabriel, who shrugged.

"Really?" Anna said, staring at Ravi. "That's how it's gonna be?"

"You'll get two practice runs," Phillips said. "The third one is the race. Ready?"

All three placed their hands on the pads and stared straight ahead at the simulator screens. In front of them was a virtual asteroid field loaded with jagged rocks of all sizes.

"Go!" STEAM exclaimed.

All three pilots shot forward . . . and all three crashed into a massive asteroid.

"Whoa," Niko said. "That's a lot harder than the orbs."

"Exactly," Phillips said. "You have to fly quickly, but with caution. Let's go again."

The screens were reset to the beginning of the course and STEAM again called out, "Go!"

This time the three pilots flew tentatively.

"The asteroids are moving!" Carly exclaimed.

"That is because asteroids move," STEAM said.

The race lasted a few seconds longer, but all three ended up crashing again.

"Extremely difficult," Siena said.

"Okay, this is it," Phillips announced. "This one counts. Ready?"

STEAM called out, "Three, two, one, GO!"

The three simulated ships shot forward, dipping and dodging, barely missing the asteroids.

"Too slow," Anna said. "You guys are flying like grannies."

Siena crashed first. Carly was right behind but Niko managed to make it all the way through to the floating red stripe that was the finish line.

"Yes!" he exclaimed.

"Don't be all proud," Anna said. "That took you like two days."

The next three to go were Dash, Gabriel, and Ravi. The results were almost exactly the same. There were quick crashes at first, followed by a very tentative final race. Ravi flew fast but crashed near the end while Gabriel and Dash made it all the way through with times better than Niko's.

Anna and Piper went last, racing head-to-head. On the first practice run, Piper crashed halfway through.

"Ouch" was all she said.

Anna, on the other hand, made it all the way through without crashing.

"That's how it's done!" she exclaimed. "I don't need any more practice, let's race!"

"I'd like to practice again," Piper said meekly.

"Knock yourself out," Anna said. She sat back and folded her arms to watch.

Piper didn't do much better on the second run. She crashed within twenty seconds.

"Maybe I'm not destined to be a pilot," she said.

"All right, let's do this!" Anna exclaimed.

"Here we go," STEAM announced. "Three, two, one . . . go!"

Anna's race was breathtaking. She flew recklessly, barely skimming past the asteroids. She cut right in front of Piper, forcing her to dodge out of the way and slam square into a speeding meteor.

"Hey!" Piper yelled.

"Ha!" Anna replied, loving it. She was a hair away from disaster with every turn but managed to make it through to the finish line with the best time of all. She threw her hands up in triumph and exclaimed, "That makes me the pilot!"

"Not exactly," Phillips said. "We'll take the best three times and you'll race each other on a much longer course."

It had come down to Anna, Dash, and Gabriel. The three strapped in and focused their attention on the screens.

"C'mon, guys!" Ravi called out. "Put her away!"

"Good luck," Dash said to his competition.

"Just fly," Anna shot back.

"This is the final race," STEAM announced. "Ready? Three, two, one, go!"

The three ships flashed forward.

Anna got off to a fast start. She was gaining experience with every passing second and managed to skirt the asteroids while often cutting it very close.

Gabriel was close behind her. He was totally focused, using his thoughts, his eyes, and his hand to finesse his ship through the danger.

Dash was a distant third. He flew with caution. His goal was to make it through without crashing.

"Woooo!" Anna screamed, loving the ride.

Gabriel fell farther behind. His chances of catching Anna grew dimmer.

"Kiss you guys good-bye!" Anna exclaimed.

Carly knelt down next to Gabriel and said, "Take your hand off the pad."

"What?" Gabriel asked while keeping his eyes focused on the screen.

"This is just a machine," she said. "You can figure this out. Use your brain."

Gabriel hesitated, gave a quick glance to Anna's screen, and saw he was hopelessly behind.

"Why not?" he said.

He took his hand off the pad.

His simulator instantly kicked into another gear. His eyes narrowed as he slipped into the zone . . . which launched him even faster. The asteroids looked like blurs as he flew by. He didn't fear hitting one because he could see which turns to make long before he got there. His analytical mind had kicked into hyperdrive.

"Wow!" Piper screamed.

Within seconds, Gabriel flashed by Anna as if she were floating still.

"No!" Anna yelled.

Gabriel shot by the finish line, the winner.

"Yeah!" he exclaimed, pumping his fist in the air.

"Told you!" Carly said as the two bumped knuckles.

"Yes, you did," Gabriel said, trying to catch his breath. "That was awesome."

Anna threw off her glasses angrily, jumped out of the sphere, and ran straight to Phillips.

"That's not fair!" she screamed, livid. "She helped him."

"Yeah," Ravi said.

"You said this was an individual test," Anna complained. "He had help."

"It was just a suggestion," Carly said defensively.

"Yeah, well, you didn't give *me* any suggestions!" Anna shot back.

"You want to run the race again?" Phillips asked Anna.

"No!" Anna exclaimed. "I want you to disqualify him."

Phillips looked at Gabriel, who sat on the edge of his simulator with his glasses off, waiting for his response.

"I'm sorry, Gabriel," Phillips said. "Anna's right. You were all supposed to race on your own. Carly's advice gave you an unfair advantage. I'm going to have to disqualify you and declare Anna the winner."

"Oh man," Gabriel said, slamming his hand against the frame.

"But Anna didn't win," Piper said.

"I sure did," Anna said, gloating.

"But you didn't finish the course," Piper said. "Somebody else did."

All eyes went to Dash's simulator monitor to see his vehicle cross the red finish line.

"Yes!" he exclaimed, throwing his hands up. "I never thought I'd get through that!"

He pulled off his glasses and looked at the others.

"Which one of you guys won?" he asked, oblivious to what had just happened.

Piper laughed.

Gabriel did too. So did Carly.

"What?" Dash asked, confused.

Anna looked ready to explode. She marched right up to Phillips and pointed a finger in his face. "We both know who the best racer was."

She stormed off, too angry to say another word.

"Well," Phillips said. "She certainly has passion."

The rest of the day was spent taking tests that weren't anywhere near as dramatic or exciting as the virtual race. The candidates were timed doing math problems and given eye tests to measure their peripheral vision and depth perception. They were hooked up to monitors that measured heart rate, oxygen intake, reaction time, and reflexes.

Dinner was once again served in the cafeteria, though it was much less elaborate than the night before. Everyone was too exhausted to talk. All they wanted was to get to their dorms and drop into bed.

"One last event for tonight," STEAM announced in the cafeteria.

The news was greeted with groans. STEAM led them back to the dorm, but rather than going to their rooms, they were brought to a corridor lined with doors. Each door had one of their names on it.

"I'm too tired for any more tests," Niko complained.

"Enter your room, please," STEAM commanded.

They all gave resigned shrugs and opened the doors, fearful of what they might encounter. Would they be poked and measured some more? Or would there be another impossible arena challenge?

Dash entered to find a simple, small room. There was a desk and chair on the far side. Sitting on the desk was a laptop. On the screen were Dash's mother and sister.

"Dash!" his sister, Abby, called out.

Dash's heart leapt. He ran for the desk and jumped into the chair, trying to get as close to the screen as possible.

"Shabby Abby!" Dash said with a laugh.

"We miss you, Dasher," Abby said. "Are you having fun at camp?"

"Fun? Uh, yeah. Sort of. Hi, Mom."

"You look tired," his mom said with worry.

"Tired? Nah. I'm exhausted! But it really is kind of fun. I won a big race today, though I don't think it meant anything. It was only because somebody messed up."

"Isn't that part of it?" Mrs. Conroy asked. "They want kids who won't mess up."

"Hadn't thought of it that way, but I'll go with that. How's everything at home?"

"We miss you," she said. "Are you okay?"

"I'm fine," Dash said seriously. "The tests and challenges make sense, but we also have to deal with a lot of drama."

"Do you want to come home?" Mrs. Conroy asked. "They said you can leave anytime."

"No way!" Dash exclaimed. "But I'll tell you, Mom, these kids are smart. I'm not so sure I belong here."

"You belong there," his mom said with confidence. "I have no doubt about that."

"Yeah, well, you're supposed to think that. It's your job."

"It's not my job," Abby said. "And I think you're going to do great."

"Thanks. The only bad thing about it is being away from home. I really miss you guys."

Mrs. Conroy had to hold back tears.

"It's okay, Mom," Dash said. "I'm not on my own. Some of the other candidates are cool."

"Glad to hear that," Mrs. Conroy said. "I want to hear all about what's—"

The computer screen went blank. The light in the cubicle went dark.

Nine o'clock.

Blackout.

8

The rest of the week played out a lot like the first few days. The competitors were given daily tests and presented with challenges that pushed their physical and mental abilities to the max. Whether it was classroom math or running sprints in the hot desert, the pressure to perform was constant.

Anna was the most focused and the most competitive. She always arrived early for classroom sessions, made sure she was at the front of every line, and never offered help to anybody else.

"It's a contest," she would say. "Why would I help the competition?"

The other seven treated the competition more as if they were on the same team. They each did their best, but they weren't above offering help or advice to the others. (Except for Ravi and Niko, who didn't help the girls much.)

A highlight of the week was when they received their Mobile Tech Band computers. "Wearable technology" was what Commander Phillips called it.

The MTB was a lightweight six-inch elastic black sleeve that slipped onto their forearms. It was like having a supercomputer wrapped snugly onto their arms. With a quick touch or a verbal command, they could tap into the massive Project Alpha database. They could also use it to communicate with each other, monitor their own vital signs, and view video on its small screen.

They were awesome.

"I'm guessing you can't pick one of these babies up at Walmart," Gabriel said.

It was this computer that gave Dash and Anna the information they needed to defeat the Raptogon in the challenge they faced together. That contest happened at the end of the first week of camp.

After triumphing against the holographic monster, Anna started talking as if she had the overall contest locked up.

"I think I know who they're going to pick," she said at dinner after the Raptogon Event.

"You mean besides you?" Ravi asked, snickering.

Everyone laughed, but it was nervous laughter because his words rang true. She was the most successful competitor. The alpha dog.

"Who?" Niko asked nervously.

Anna looked the group over, meeting their awkward gazes, enjoying the fact that they all knew she was the front-runner.

"If I was choosing the team," she finally said after holding them all in suspense, "I'd take Gabriel, Niko, and Siena."

Those three let out a collective breath.

"You don't think the rest of us are any good?" Carly asked.

"No, you've all got skills. But you're too . . . cautious. I want people who aren't afraid to follow me when common sense says it's better to play it safe. I don't see that with you guys. You're just too . . ."

"Smart?" Dash asked. "Is that the word you're looking for?"

Anna shot him a scornful look.

"No, the word I was going for was . . . *scared.*"

She got up and headed for the door.

"Remember what I said" were her parting words. "To make this team, you gotta stand out and be special. Step it up, people, or go home."

The others waited until she was out of earshot before speaking.

"She's right, you know," Siena said. "She is a lock for the crew. The rest of us better find a way to get along with her. Good night."

She got up and left.

Ravi stood and said, "Way too much drama going on here. I'm going to conference with my folks. Then I'm going to meditate with Niko and figure out how we can turn Anna into less of a tool."

Niko joined him and said, "What? No we're not."

"It was a joke. Jeez."

The two took off.

"I'm not scared," Piper said, then winked and smiled. "Except maybe of Anna."

She sped out of the room leaving Dash, Gabriel, and Carly.

"I'm with Piper," Gabriel said. "Imagine being on a ship for a year with her? Yikes."

"Seriously," Carly added. "She's not exactly a people person."

Dash shrugged and said, "Yeah, well, let's hope we get the chance to worry about that. Good night, guys."

As he got up, Carly gave Gabriel a shove and motioned with her eyes toward Dash.

Gabriel nodded. "Hey, Dash, you got a minute?"

Dash sat back down. "Sure, what's up?"

"I think they're going to name the crew soon," Gabriel said. "I mean, how much more can they learn about us?"

"True," Dash said. "Hard to believe it's almost over."

"Or about to begin," Carly said.

She looked at Gabriel and once again implored him with her eyes to talk to Dash.

"What's going on?" Dash asked with a curious chuckle.

"We . . . discovered something the other day," Gabriel said. "You know those blackouts every night? They're not real. They've got monster generators that make more than enough power for this camp, but every night they shut them down and tell us we've been blacked out."

"But they keep one running," Carly said. "So they've still got power. We've seen the control room and watched them power down."

"Why do you think they're doing that?" Dash asked.

"Exactly!" Gabriel blurted out, a bit too loud. "How can we trust them to shoot us into space if they're not being totally honest with us?"

Dash frowned and dropped his head to concentrate.

"Do the other guys know?" he asked.

"No, just us," Gabriel replied. "And now you."

"What do you think we should do?" Carly asked.

Dash's mind spun, trying to calculate the possibilities.

"Nothing," he said. "Not yet, anyway. Maybe there's a good reason they're not telling us. Hopefully one of us will be on the crew and then we can ask about it. If none of us are chosen, we'll let the others know and they can deal."

"It's not cool that they're keeping secrets from us," Carly said.

"I have a feeling there's a whole lot of stuff they're not telling us," Dash said.

"You do?" Carly asked, wide-eyed.

"Absolutely. This whole project has been top secret. Heck, nobody in the world knew they had the technology to send people into deep space until they announced the competition. Once the crew is chosen, that's when we should start asking questions."

Gabriel and Carly both nodded in agreement.

"So why did you tell me?" Dash asked.

Carly said, "Because we thought you'd know the right thing to do."

"There you are!" STEAM announced as he scurried into the room.

The three kids stiffened up as if they'd been caught doing something wrong.

"Bedtime," STEAM announced. "You need rest. Huge day tomorrow! Yes sir!"

"What's tomorrow?" Gabriel asked.

"Final challenge. A big one! Very exciting, yes sir!"

"Wait, final challenge?" Dash asked. "Does that mean—?"

"Yes," STEAM said. "The crew will be selected tomorrow night."

9

Commander Phillips and STEAM faced all eight candidates, who stood at one end of the giant tent.

"You have all proven yourselves worthy," Phillips announced. "Unfortunately, only four can fly."

"So this is our last test," Siena said.

"It is," Phillips replied. "You are all still in the running, so don't even think about giving it less than your best. This last challenge could change everything."

Dash saw movement on the catwalk above.

A young blond man with a golden retriever stood looking down on the group.

"Who's that?" Dash asked.

Phillips glanced up.

"One of my team," he answered dismissively. "I haven't been the only one observing you."

"So what's this challenge?" Anna asked impatiently.

"It's very simple," Phillips replied. "Your goal is to make it from here to the far side of the tent."

"That's it?" Gabriel asked. "It's just a race?"

"It is," Phillips said. "With one small wrinkle."

Phillips raised his hand and the tent went pitch-dark.

"Ooh, a race in the dark," Anna said sarcastically. "Spooky."

Slowly, the lights began to rise again, revealing that the space had completely transformed.

"No way," Niko said with a gasp.

"This is impossible," Siena said, wide-eyed.

The space had become an elaborate steampunk world with massive brass boilers, miles of pipes snaking up the walls and across the ceiling, and conveyor belts that moved on multiple levels, transporting machine parts throughout the dark, industrial-looking environment. A steady hissing sound filled the air as the riveted joints let out occasional blasts of steam. The floor had become a massive, living checkerboard with images of two-foot square brass plates that moved randomly about.

"This is the Meta Prime Event," Phillips announced.

"I feel like I'm dreaming," Dash said in awe.

"You're not imagining this," Phillips said. "But it isn't real. The entire Meta Prime arena is computer-generated, like the Raptogon."

A small machine part jumped off a conveyor belt, landed on a brass floor square, then bounced off to land on another square. It rode that square to the far side of the floor and jumped off, disappearing into the maze of machinery.

"What the heck was that?" Gabriel asked.

"A robot," Phillips replied. "That's what this virtual machine manufactures. There are robots scattered throughout the factory who are programmed to protect it from intruders."

"And we're the intruders?" Dash asked.

"Exactly," Phillips replied. "Now you can see how challenging it will be to make your way through. Beneath those brass floor plate images is nothing. Or the illusion of nothing. If a plate slides out from under you, it's as if you fall off and die."

"Wait, what?" Anna exclaimed.

"You don't actually die," Phillips said quickly. "Think of it as a video game."

He walked into the hologram and stepped onto one of the brass plates. A moment later, it flew out from under him, but Phillips didn't fall. It looked as though he was standing in midair.

"It's a projection," he explained. "When you lose, you go back to the beginning and start over again. If one of the robots hunts you down and tags you with its laser, you die and start over. If you fall into the abyss, you die and start over. If you get swallowed by the machine—"

"You die and start over," Gabriel said. "This is impossible."

"It will take some ingenuity to make your way through," Phillips said.

"And if we lose, we might not get picked for the crew," Ravi said.

"Yeah," Niko added. "We die and don't start over."

Phillips shrugged. "Use your heads. We're looking to see who is clever enough to avoid the dangers and find their way through to the other side. Questions?"

"Yes," Dash said. "What's this weird fake factory got to do with a mission to outer space?"

"Good question," Phillips said. "The answer will wait until—"

"Until we're on the crew," Carly said.

Phillips nodded. "Any other questions?"

"When do we start?" Anna asked.

"Right now!" Phillips announced.

Anna instantly took off running into the "factory." She leapt onto a brass floor plate, then another, trying to hopscotch across. When she jumped onto a fourth, the plate shot out from under her to reveal the bottomless abyss.

"Ahhh!" she screamed, expecting to fall.

She stood seemingly in midair and had to stomp on the floor to prove it was still there.

"This is crazy!" she exclaimed.

A moment later, an alarm sounded and she was hit with a dozen red laser lights.

"That means you died," Phillips called out.

Anna huffed and jogged back to the others across the projection.

"Yeah, I figured that," she said, snarky.

"You can see how tricky this is," Phillips said. "This challenge isn't about speed or agility; it's about using your head. Good luck."

With that, Phillips strode to the door and left.

Everyone stared at the impossible factory, each wondering how they could possibly defeat the hologram checkerboard puzzle.

"I'm just gonna go!" Niko exclaimed, and jumped onto a brass square.

He made it to one, then the next, then the third. He made it halfway to the first large boiler and jumped onto a fixed "girder" that spanned the floor.

"I got this!" he yelled.

A moment later, a small robot that was a cross between E.T. and a toaster oven zipped along the girder he was standing on, stopped two feet from him, and hit him with a green laser beam. The alarm sounded and Niko was bathed in the red lasers.

The robot retreated along the beam.

"Oh man," Niko said, jogging back to the group. "This is tough."

"It can't be impossible," Dash said. "Or it wouldn't be one of the challenges."

Gabriel stepped away from the group and stared at the incredible contraption, squinting in concentration. He watched the timing of the floor tiles closely, as well as the movement of the robots that zipped through intermittently.

"There must be a pattern," Siena said.

Dash took a shot. He jumped from floor plate to floor plate, trying to keep away from the wide-open center and stay closer to the machines that ringed the checkerboard. He made it to one of the conveyor belts and crouched down behind it to hide from the guard robots. But one of the little guards appeared on the conveyor directly over his head, hopped down, and zapped him. Alarm. Lasers. Done.

"Wow" was all Dash could say as he jogged back to the start.

One by one, they tried different routes, but each time they either had a brass plate zip out from under them or were shot by robots.

Piper rolled her chair onto one of the plates but instantly lost when the plate slid out from under her.

"This isn't fair," Piper said. "No way I can get across."

"No way I'm giving up!" Ravi said with determination.

Seconds later, he got zapped. Again.

Dash was about to give it another shot when he spied Gabriel standing alone, still squinting at the complicated hologram. Dash walked up to him and said, "Aren't you going to try?"

"I've been looking for a pattern," Gabriel said with a frown. "Every time I think I've got it, it changes. The robots are a wild card. They react based on what we do, so it's different every time."

Carly joined them and said, "Maybe that's the challenge. They want to see how we deal with a contest that's unwinnable."

Dash's mind raced; an idea was forming. "Or maybe we just have to figure out new rules."

"What does that mean?" Carly asked.

"This isn't a real machine," he said thoughtfully. "It's generated by a computer. So what we really have to beat is the computer."

Anna was down on her belly, crawling from floor plate to floor plate, hoping that she wouldn't be spotted by one of the annoying little robots. She rolled onto a plate . . . and came face to face with one of the little monsters. Zap. Alarm. Done.

She stood up and headed back to the start when she spotted Dash, Carly, and Gabriel talking. She changed course and walked to them.

"You're not gonna get anywhere just standing there," she said.

Gabriel threw up his hands in frustration and said, "We're not gonna get anywhere no matter what we do. There's no way to win this thing. You're all just spinning your wheels. I am outta here."

He stormed off, headed for the door.

"Gabriel, wait," Carly said, and ran after him. "You can't give up."

Gabriel kept going and blasted out the door with Carly right behind him.

Anna said, "Guess the pressure finally got to them. Too bad. I wanted Gabriel on my crew."

"Guess you have to pick somebody else," Dash said.

Anna scoffed. "Yeah, well, it won't be you."

"Darn," Dash said.

Anna backed away from him and jogged to the hologram.

Siena, Ravi, and Niko continued making vain attempts to hopscotch across and dodge the robots, but died each time. The little robots seemed to take joy in gunning them down. Some would spin happily afterward, or let out a bright mechanical twerp. It only added to everyone's frustration.

"This is stupid!" Ravi yelled out in anger. "I hate those little creeps."

Piper sat on the edge of the game, looking sour.

"Do me a favor?" Dash said as he walked up to her.

"Sure, what?"

"Give me a ride to the other side?"

Piper gave him a curious look.

"I'm serious," Dash said.

"You realize that won't work," Piper said. "I tried."

"Maybe you should try again."

Piper shrugged and said, "Sure, why not. I'm not doing anything else."

Dash walked to the edge of the hologram and motioned for Piper to join him. She rolled the chair over and stopped on the very edge of the illusion.

"Let's go," she said.

"Not yet," Dash said.

He watched as Niko was chased down by a robot. Ravi ran behind the little machine, hoping not to be seen. It didn't work. The robot spun and shot Ravi, then spun back and nailed Niko. Double fail. Both howled with exasperation as the robot squealed with delight.

"Did Gabriel and Carly give up?" Piper asked.

"Sort of."

"How can you sort of give up?"

"We didn't like the rules of this game, so we decided to change them."

Dash's Mobile Tech Band sprang to life. Carly's image appeared on the small screen.

"Ready?" Carly asked.

"Almost," Dash said.

He stepped onto the back of Piper's chair.

"Okay," Dash said to Carly. "Anytime."

"What are you guys doing?" Piper asked, totally confused.

Carly said, "You're good to go in three . . . two . . . one . . ."

Suddenly, the lights went out and the tent was thrown into pitch darkness.

"What the heck?" Anna called out from somewhere.

Dash held out his Mobile Tech Band and triggered the flashlight mechanism. A beam of light shot from his wrist, which he focused on the floor in front of them.

"Step on it," Dash commanded.

Piper laughed and jammed the wheelchair into gear. They took off with a lurch and sped across the floor of the arena. The hologram of the machine was gone. All that lay ahead was an empty floor . . . and the finish line.

"What's going on?" Niko yelled.

Dash and Piper zoomed by Ravi, who stood there in shock.

"No!" Anna yelled. "No way!"

She took off running after them, but it was too late. Piper opened the throttle and the two sped across the empty floor, easily pulling away from Anna.

"Yaaaaa!" Piper screamed with sheer exhilaration.

"Wooooo!" Dash yelled.

When they reached the far wall, he jumped out and touched it as Piper spun the wheelchair in a mini victory lap.

"No way, this doesn't count!" Anna yelled as she ran up. "You can't win because the power failed."

Niko, Ravi, and Siena ran up, breathless.

"What the heck happened?" Ravi asked.

"They got lucky is what happened," Anna said. "That's not a victory."

"Nothing went wrong with the hologram," Dash said. "We took it out of the equation."

"Uh . . . what?" Niko asked, confused.

The lights suddenly came back on to reveal the vast empty tent. The hologram was no more.

Standing in front of them were Commander Phillips and STEAM.

"I want a do-over," Anna said.

"Why's that?" Phillips asked.

Anna was so angry her head seemed ready to explode. "Because they didn't beat the machine."

"Well, actually they did," Phillips said. "Just not the way that I expected."

The door from the hangar opened and a soldier wearing desert-camouflage fatigues stepped in. He was followed close behind by Carly and Gabriel. The soldier strode right to Phillips and gave him a quick salute.

"That could have been a disaster, Commander," he said.

"Understood," Phillips said. "Leave them with me."

The soldier turned and strode off as Gabriel and Carly joined the group. Both were trying hard not to smile.

"Thanks!" Carly called to the soldier.

Gabriel went right to Dash and they exchanged high fives.

"Is there an explanation for this?" Siena asked.

"That's what we want to know," Gabriel said. "You know those blackouts every night? They aren't real. They've got huge generators that power the whole camp but they've been shutting them down and telling us we're blacked out. Why is that, Commander?"

All eyes went to Phillips.

"Is that true?" Siena asked.

"It is," Phillips replied. "The fact that we power down every night is voluntary. If the rest of the country is dark, we should be too. It's the right thing to do."

"But you're still generating power, even at night," Carly said. "Why?"

"There are facilities here that would be irreparably damaged if they were totally cut off. That would jeopardize the entire mission and we can't risk that. When the final crew is chosen, you'll see exactly what I mean."

"Why couldn't you just tell us that?" Gabriel asked.

"I understand your concern," Phillips said. "Please know that you are all still on a need-to-know basis . . . until you need to know."

"What's all that got to do with the hologram?" Anna asked.

Commander Phillips looked at Gabriel and Carly.

"The challenge was to beat the program and get to the far side of the arena," Carly said. "Nobody said how we had to do it."

"We found the base's generators last week and saw how they were powered down," Gabriel said, matter of fact. "It was simple. No power, no hologram."

"It was Dash's idea," Carly said.

Anna shot a scathing look at Dash, who shrugged modestly.

"That's cheating!" she exclaimed.

"I don't agree," Phillips said. "The task was to find a way to outwit the program and get to the far side. That was accomplished by Dash and Piper, with assistance from Gabriel and Carly." Phillips faced Gabriel and Carly and added, "But I would appreciate it if you left the running of Base Ten to the camp personnel."

"You got it, Commander," Gabriel said, and saluted Phillips.

"Congratulations to all four of you," Phillips said. "Nicely done."

Anna wanted to argue further, but she knew she was beaten.

"That officially concludes the competition," Phillips announced. "We'll make the crew choices tonight and give you the news tomorrow. You've earned the right to celebrate. Head back to the dorm. We've got a little something planned for you."

Phillips turned and walked off with STEAM.

"I don't believe it," Anna said, grumbling. "I didn't know it was okay to cheat."

"We didn't cheat," Dash said. "We worked together to solve a problem."

Anna stalked toward Dash, staring him right in the eyes. Dash didn't flinch, though a bead of sweat appeared on his forehead.

"You were smart," she said, growling under her breath. "But you gotta be more than smart to win this competition."

The two stood nose to nose.

A dog's bark broke the tense silence.

All eyes went skyward to see the golden retriever looking down on them with its tail wagging. The blond young man was gone.

Anna broke away from Dash and stormed off.

Niko and Ravi headed off too.

Siena approached the others.

"Ingenious," she said. "I wish I had thought of that myself."

She followed the others.

"Thanks for including me," Piper said to Dash.

"Don't thank me. Without you, Anna would have beaten me to the finish line. So thank *you.*"

"I don't know who's going to win this competition," Carly said. "But that was awesome."

"Yeah, it was," Gabriel said. "Now if we don't all get kicked out of here for nearly destroying the base, we might have a shot at this."

10

"I'm not looking forward to this," Carly said as she and Piper approached the foyer of their dorm building.

"Seriously," Piper said. "I'm too tired to do any more challenges today."

"Welcome!" STEAM exclaimed as he hurried up to them. "Enjoy. You have earned it. Yes sir!"

"Earned what?" Carly asked.

Suddenly, thumping dance music kicked in, making the floor vibrate.

"It is a party!" STEAM said, and led them into the foyer.

The two stood there, wide-eyed to see that the space was decorated for a celebration. Orange and blue balloons covered the ceiling. Multicolored crepe-paper streamers hung down to hide the drab walls. A long table was loaded with bowls of chips and candy. Another held a variety of juices and sodas.

It looked like a festive school dance.

Except nobody was having fun.

Siena sat by herself, reading.

The boys all surrounded the snack table.

Anna wasn't even there.

STEAM swung his arms and jumped from foot to foot in a strange attempt to dance. It looked more like he had short-circuited a critical movement function.

Everyone rolled their eyes and turned away from the robot.

STEAM gave up, dropped his head, and went back to pouring soda.

Carly and Piper approached Siena, making it official that the boys were on one side of the room and the girls on the other.

"I don't think reading is allowed at a party," Carly said with a smile.

"I'm doing research on the changes in physiology of the human body during long periods of space flight," Siena said.

Carly shot Piper a look and said, "Oh, in that case. That's allowed."

"Thank you," Siena said, and went back to reading.

"I was kidding!" Carly said, and took the book from her. "Take a break—we earned it."

"If you insist," Siena said with a sigh. "What should we do?"

Carly looked around at the overdone yet earnest decorations.

"They tried to make this look like a dance, so let's dance," she said.

She took Siena by the hand and pulled her out of her seat.

"You too," Carly said to Piper, and pushed her wheelchair into the center of the room.

The three faced each other and started bouncing to the music. Siena had no rhythm and looked completely uncomfortable. Piper laughed and rocked in her seat. Carly liked to dance and spun around the other two.

The boys watched with looks that said they would rather be fighting another Raptogon than venturing out to dance.

"This is a strange end to a very strange week," Niko said. "It's weird to think that some of us are going home tomorrow."

"To be honest, I miss my family," Ravi said. "I want to be on the crew, but going home wouldn't be a horrible thing."

"I miss my family too," Gabriel said. "But I really want this. And they could use the ten million bucks."

"What about you, Dash?" Niko asked.

Dash thought hard before answering. "I guess I'm hoping if we don't make the crew, there might still be some way we can help with the mission."

"Yeah," Ravi said. "Like teaching Anna to lighten up."

"Look!" Gabriel said.

STEAM was between the three girls, whirling and dancing . . . badly.

"I'm glad somebody's having fun," Niko said.

STEAM danced his way over to the boys.

"Oh no," Ravi said. "Don't even think about it."

"But it is a party. Enjoy yourselves. Make my day," STEAM said.

"You go ahead and knock yourself out," Ravi said.

"Dash," STEAM said. "Please go to the supply room and retrieve a few liters of soda?"

"Absolutely," Dash said, and hurried off, relieved that he didn't have to dance. "Don't hurt yourself, Steamer."

STEAM gave him a pistol shot with his little mechanical finger, then turned to the other guys.

All three turned their backs on him.

"You are party poopers," STEAM said.

Dash left the foyer and walked down the long corridor that led to the supply room. Inside was Commander Phillips sitting on top of a table.

"Oh, hi," Dash said with surprise. "You should come to the party. It's really . . . uh . . ."

"Boring?"

Dash shrugged and smiled. "Nice try, though."

"Something's come up," Phillips said gravely.

"Oh," Dash said. "I guess I wasn't really sent here to get soda."

"There's a problem."

Dash stood silently, waiting for the worst . . . and got it.

"It's you," Phillips said.

"Is this because I had the idea for shutting down the generators? That was a mistake. I won't do anything like that again."

"It wasn't a mistake. It was brilliant."

"Oh. So then what's the problem?"

"You're twelve and a half years old."

Dash stared at Phillips, uncomprehending. "Not getting that."

"We thought you were twelve," Phillips explained. "Somewhere along the line, your birthday was entered incorrectly into our system and you're actually six months older than we thought. We just realized it today."

"Still don't get why that's a problem," Dash said.

Phillips ran his hands through his hair and took a deep, troubled breath.

"Why do you think we're putting together a crew of such young people?" he asked.

"I thought it had something to do with adults not being able to physically handle the stress of the flight, or something."

"That's exactly right. We've developed a revolutionary propulsion system that allows the ship to make jumps not only through space but also time. It's how we can send the crew to such a far-flung location. Without this propulsion system, the journey out and back could take years. Decades. Now we can get a crew out and back in one year."

"So why is my age a problem?" Dash asked.

"The biological component of the system wreaks havoc on the metabolisms of older astronauts. Anyone over the age of fourteen is a liability, a risk."

"Oh" was all Dash managed to say.

"The schedule calls for six months of training before launch. The trip itself will take a year. That means—"

"That means I'll hit the danger age before we get back," Dash said soberly.

Phillips looked down and kicked at the floor.

"How accurate is this?" Dash asked.

"Enough that we can't risk it," Phillips replied. "Simply put, you could die."

Dash's heart sank.

"So that's it. I'm out," he said, trying not to let his voice quiver.

"It seems so," Phillips said.

"Wow" was all Dash could say as tears formed in his eyes. "I guess I never had a shot."

"I'm sorry," Phillips said with genuine regret. "I wish we had known earlier."

"Any chance this is a mistake?" Dash asked with a touch of desperation.

"No," Phillips said.

Dash wiped his eyes and picked up a couple of bottles of soda.

"Okay, then. I should get these back to the party."

He turned for the door, then stopped and said, "Would I have made it?"

"I don't know if this is going to make you feel better or worse, but of all the candidates, you were the only slam dunk. You brought this team together, Dash. More than once. That was one of the qualities we were looking for and you exceeded every expectation. I hope that means something to you."

"It does. Thanks. I, uh, I'm not going to tell anybody. I don't want this to turn into a pity party."

"I understand. Nobody will know until tomorrow."

Dash gave a nod of thanks and left the room. He walked slowly back toward the party. It was over. Any hope of being part of the greatest adventure in the history of mankind was gone. He wasn't going to save the world. He wasn't going to give his mother ten million dollars. He was going home. Dash reached the door to the foyer and looked out at the group.

The guys were still hovering around the food.

Carly and Piper chatted on the opposite side of the room.

Siena had gone back to reading.

It was hard to celebrate when every last one of them had

their stomach in a knot, thinking about what the next day would bring.

Dash looked at them each in turn, wondering who would be going up and who would feel as badly as he did.

He stood up straight, took a deep breath, and shouted out, "Hey, what kind of party is this?"

He ran into the room, shaking the bottle of soda.

"Let's have some fun!" he exclaimed as he twisted off the cap. A spray of soda flew, dousing the guys.

"Yeah!" Carly cheered, jumped up, and ran for the soda table. She grabbed another bottle of soda, shook it up, and let it erupt all over the others.

Siena hid her book under the cushion of a sofa for protection.

"Oh yeah!" Gabriel shouted. "It is so on!" He went for the food, grabbed handfuls of M&M's, and whipped them at Dash.

Dash retaliated by dumping a bowl of Cheez-Its over Gabriel's head.

The party quickly degenerated into a raucous, messy celebration of food fighting and fun. Everyone battled everyone else while laughing, throwing, and even dancing.

Anna watched the mayhem from the far end of the foyer with her arms folded. STEAM scampered over to her with soda dripping from his big eyes.

"Join the fun," STEAM said.

Anna shook her head. "They don't want me there."

"Yes they do," STEAM argued.

"No, a leader shouldn't let her guard down like that. Good night."

She turned her back on the group and headed for her room.

Behind her, the battle raged.

The tension was gone.

Ravi filled his mouth with soda and sprayed it at Niko, who was disgusted and laughed hysterically at the same time. Dash couldn't stop laughing either, until he looked past Niko and saw STEAM.

The little robot was looking at him with his oversized mechanical eyes.

STEAM knew the truth. If it was possible for a robot to show sympathy, STEAM was doing it. Dash gave him a small smile and a shrug of resignation.

STEAM gave Dash a salute, then picked up a cup of punch and tossed it at Ravi. "We will party like it is 1999!" STEAM exclaimed.

"I have no idea what that means!" Ravi yelled back.

The party raged on.

Tomorrow the real show would begin.

11

Base Ten felt like a carnival.

A sea of folding chairs faced the doors of the largest hangar on the base. A military band played patriotic tunes. Television cameras were everywhere, all focused on a stage that was set up in front of the giant hangar. On stage sat a podium and four chairs: one for each of the soon-to-be-announced Project Alpha crew.

The seats filled quickly with Base Ten personnel. The press section overflowed with eager reporters. The front row had seven chairs roped off and a space for one wheelchair, waiting for the stars of the hour.

At ten o'clock sharp, the band finished playing "The Stars and Stripes Forever" as a bus with darkened windows pulled up to the side of the stage. The bus door opened, and Commander Phillips stepped off and climbed the long ramp that led to the top of the platform.

The crowd was totally silent as Phillips walked up to the microphone.

"The dream is finally a reality," he began, his amplified voice booming across the base. "We are about to begin the final preparations that will send four brave astronauts to the far end of the galaxy and back."

The hundreds of people in attendance, and the support team for Project Alpha, broke out into thunderous applause. Even the reporters applauded.

"I have no doubt that we will rise to the challenge. We must. Too much is at stake. As we have said so many times, failure is not an option. And we . . . will . . . not . . . fail."

The crowd once again broke into applause. Phillips raised his hands to quiet them.

"You should save your applause for the eight exceptional young people who have volunteered for the mission. They have put in long hours of hard work and gone through strenuous testing. They represent the best and the brightest that our world has produced. I present to you the eight finalists of Project Alpha."

The door of the bus opened and the eight candidates marched out wearing crisp, clean orange-and-blue training uniforms.

The audience cheered. The band kicked in with a rousing version of "Off We Go into the Wild Blue Yonder" as Anna led them past the rows of ecstatic soldiers and straight to their seats in front.

Anna waved to the crowd like an Olympic champion. Ravi did too. Siena looked awkward and embarrassed. Piper beamed a big, happy smile. Dash was last, putting on a good face. He was the only one who felt no pressure because he already knew his fate. He smiled and waved anyway because that's what he was asked to do.

Their images were being broadcast throughout the United

States and around the globe. Hope for the future of the world would rest on the shoulders of four of these young astronauts. They were heroes before ever setting foot inside a space vehicle.

They reached their places, gave one last wave to the crowd, and took their seats.

Phillips leaned into the mike and said, "That wonderful reception was well deserved. Though only four of these young people will fly, they are all equally qualified."

Dash held his head high.

Phillips said, "The choice was difficult, but ultimately we assembled a crew we felt would make the best team. The success of this mission will not rest on the abilities of any one individual. It will be the sum of the parts that will make it to the Source, and bring it back."

That brought the people to their feet again with thunderous applause.

"To the four who will be going home," Phillips said, "please know that we honor you today as well, and we are all grateful for your sacrifice and your hard work. Once the crew is announced, I'll bring you to the bus to begin your journey home. Please, remember one very important thing: you will officially become alternates. If anything happens to one of our principal crew members during training, you may be called upon to take their place."

The group exchanged hopeful looks, realizing that even if they weren't chosen, all might not be lost.

Except for Dash.

"Now, let's get to the reason we're here," Phillips said with enthusiasm. "When I call your name, please stand and make your way up to the platform. Understood?"

The kids all nodded or gave a thumbs-up.

Piper leaned closer to Dash and whispered, "Good luck."

Dash gave her a sad smile and said, "Thanks. You too."

The rest sat up straight, their eyes fixed squarely on Commander Phillips.

Phillips didn't need to open an envelope or read from a list. He knew his crew.

"The first Project Alpha crew member is . . . Carly Diamond."

The crowd burst into applause.

"Yes!" Carly squealed with delight, pumping her fist.

The other seven candidates applauded, though the pressure on each of them had just notched up.

Carly leaned into Gabriel and said, "See you up there."

She sprinted up the ramp to meet Phillips. The two shook hands, then Carly turned and waved to the crowd and the cameras ecstatically.

The audience's excitement quickly shifted from joy to anticipation as they quieted down to wait for the next name.

Phillips announced, "The next crew member is . . . Gabriel Parker."

Again the crowd erupted with applause.

Again Carly pumped her fist and shouted, "Yes!"

Gabriel stood slowly, stunned. He truly did not expect to be chosen, especially after the stunt he pulled by shutting down the base's generators.

Niko and Ravi pounded him on the back to congratulate him.

"Makes absolute sense," Siena said.

Anna applauded politely.

"Go!" Dash urged.

Gabriel snapped into the moment. He gave Piper and Dash a high five, then jogged up the ramp. After a quick handshake from Phillips, he joined Carly.

"I told you," she whispered.

Gabriel couldn't stop grinning.

The applause died and Phillips stepped back to the microphone.

"Third up is . . . Piper Williams."

There was a mixture of surprised gasps and huge cheers.

"Me?" she said to nobody. "Did he say my name?"

"Yeah, he did," Dash said with a huge, beaming smile. "I knew you'd be chosen. Get up there!"

Piper put her chair in gear and headed toward the ramp.

"No way," Anna said, stunned.

Ravi leaned into Niko and said, "Guess that means we're going home."

Niko shrugged. He felt the same way. The last spot would certainly go to Anna or Dash.

"Well," Siena said, "this is disappointing."

Piper sped onto the stage and straight to Phillips.

"Thank you," Piper said with tears in her eyes.

"Don't thank me, you earned it," Phillips replied.

Piper wheeled herself next to Carly and Gabriel, who greeted her with warm hugs.

Three-quarters of the crew was set.

The crowd quieted.

Dash had trouble swallowing. His quest was about to

officially come to an end. He looked across to Niko, Anna, Siena, and Ravi, who stared up at Phillips with anticipation. Anna was the calmest of the four. She felt no pressure.

Dash just wanted it to be over.

"Besides announcing the name of the final crew member," Phillips said, "I'm also announcing that based on their exceptional performance in this competition, this candidate will become the commander of the Alpha team."

Anna sat up a little straighter.

Ravi leaned into Niko and whispered, "Now I *know* we're done."

Phillips continued, "This candidate has demonstrated the kind of resourcefulness, intelligence, and ingenuity that will be critical in helping the crew deal with challenges both expected and unexpected. We have complete confidence that under this candidate's leadership, the Alpha mission will be successful in bringing the Source back to Earth."

The crowd remained silent. Nobody was breathing.

"The final crew member and the commander of the Alpha team is—"

"Dash Conroy!" Carly shouted out.

The outburst caught Phillips by surprise. He didn't know how to react.

"Dash Conroy!" Piper shouted.

A low murmur went through the crowd.

Niko and Ravi looked at Anna, who seemed ready to explode with anger. She stared straight at Carly and Piper. If looks could kill, Project Alpha was going to need two new crew members.

"Dash Conroy!" Gabriel exclaimed.

Carly and Gabriel stood on either side of Piper, holding hands in a show of solidarity.

"Be careful how you handle this," Siena whispered to Anna. "You're going to have to win them over."

"Uh-uh," Anna said, gritting her teeth. "They're going to have to win *me* over."

Phillips watched the three for a moment, shaking his head in amazement.

"C'mon, Commander," Gabriel said. "You know it's gotta be."

Phillips turned back to the mike.

The crowd quieted once again.

Anna shook off her anger, sat up straight, and put a smile back on her face.

"This final choice was a difficult one," Phillips announced. "But ultimately we are one hundred percent confident in our selection. The final crew member and the commander of the Alpha crew is . . . Dash Conroy."

Anna made a move to stand, but froze instead.

"What?" she exclaimed with surprise.

Dash was even more shocked.

Niko and Ravi clapped him on the back.

"We knew it'd be you, man," Ravi said.

"Good luck, Dash," Niko said.

As Dash went for the stage, Niko looked at Ravi and said, "I thought we had a plan."

"Should have been us, man," Ravi said, shaking his head. "Should have been us."

Anna looked ready to jump out of her skin. She moved to stand up, but Siena put her arm out to stop her.

"Don't be foolish," Siena said in such a forceful, confident tone that Anna actually stopped.

Dash couldn't move his feet. This made no sense.

As the crowd cheered ecstatically, Ravi pushed Dash to get moving. On the stage Carly, Gabriel, and Piper were cheering and whistling for joy.

Dash walked up the ramp in a daze and went right for Phillips.

The two shook hands and leaned in to one another.

"I don't get it," Dash whispered.

"We'll talk," Phillips said, and directed him toward the others.

He joined hands with them and the four raised their arms in triumph.

"Ladies and gentlemen and people of the world," Phillips announced, "I present to you the Voyagers."

The crowd jumped to their feet. Even the reporters, who normally looked at events with cold indifference, stood and cheered.

The other candidates stood and applauded. All but Anna. She fidgeted anxiously.

Phillips said, "Please give a final show of appreciation to the four alternates who will be waiting in the wings should one of our crew be unable to fly."

As the band kicked in with another tune, Phillips left the stage and walked quickly down the ramp and directly to the four alternates in the front row. He gestured for them to follow him.

Anna looked to the far side of the stage to see the bus door opening. It made her stomach drop. She had planned on leaving Base Ten on a spaceship, not a bus.

She stormed ahead of the group and climbed aboard. The others walked with Phillips and gave a quick wave back to the crowd before boarding.

Phillips entered after them and the door immediately closed. Once it sealed shut, the music and the raucous cheers were reduced to a muted hum.

"This is wrong!" Anna exclaimed, fighting back tears. "How can you say Conroy would be a better commander than me? I won two of the major competitions and would have won a third if Gabriel and Carly hadn't cheated."

"This isn't about any one individual," Phillips said. "The choices reflect what we believe will make the best team. The mission is going to require a variety of skills, plus we felt strongly about selecting the candidates who demonstrated the ability to work together."

"So it didn't matter that I nailed every test?" Anna asked, indignant.

"Every test but one," Phillips replied. "You weren't collaborative."

Anna opened her mouth to argue, but stopped. Phillips was right, and she knew it.

"Thanks for the chance, Commander," Niko said, shaking his hand. "Good luck."

Ravi put out his hand to shake as well. "Yeah. Don't mess up."

"Thank you for the opportunity," Siena said. "It was enlightening."

Anna stood back, sulking.

"Remember," Phillips added, "you may still get the call. It's a long time until launch day."

"I don't do second string," Anna mumbled.

"Well, you don't have to make that choice now," Phillips said. "Next stop is the airport for your flights home. Safe journey. We'll keep in touch."

The bus door opened, and Phillips stepped back into the music and the roar of the crowd.

"Let's get out of here," Anna said, and fell down into her seat.

The bus rolled, headed for the exit of Base Ten. Many in the crowd waved to them, but most had their eyes focused on the stage and the young astronauts who had just become the four most famous people on Earth.

Phillips jogged back up onto the stage. He gestured for the crew to sit, then held up his hands to quiet the audience.

"I want to take a moment to briefly outline the Voyagers' mission," he announced, focused directly at the television cameras.

"I'm sure many of you watching today are skeptical about deep-space travel. You're wondering how it was possible for us to have developed this technology. I'm about to show you something that will put your concerns to rest and help you believe that a better tomorrow is coming."

The sound of multiple hydraulic engines began to grow, giving off a deep, throaty rumble that echoed over the desert floor. All eyes went to the roof of the football-field-sized hangar, where giant ceiling panels were opening up to the sky.

Dash, Piper, Carly, and Gabriel turned in their chairs to watch the show.

"What's going on?" Piper asked Dash.

"You're asking the wrong guy," Dash said. "I still don't even know why I'm sitting here."

All television cameras focused on the roof of the hangar.

The thunderous motorized sound grew louder as something began to rise up from inside the building. Something big. Carly, Dash, and Gabriel stood up, and Piper spun her chair.

"Is that what I think it is?" Gabriel said in awe.

"Ladies and gentlemen," Phillips announced with pride, "the vehicle that will take our Voyagers team to the stars."

With that, the roof panels dropped down, revealing the vessel that had risen from within.

There was no mistaking what it was.

A spaceship.

There was no applause. Most of the people there had seen it before. They had worked on it for years.

The reveal was for the benefit of the rest of the world.

The ship was enormous, taking up the entire platform that rose out of the hangar. It stood five stories high with a gleaming silver body that was oval-shaped and came to a slightly pointed nose. It rested on an enormous black ring. Multicolored running lights winked on and off across its skin, showing that the vehicle was alive and powered.

"People of the United States, of the world, of the planet Earth, I proudly present to you . . . the *Cloud Leopard.*"

The crowd finally erupted with cheers of pride.

The four crew members could only gaze at the ship with their mouths open, stunned.

"This suddenly got very real," Carly said with wide-eyed wonder.

"Yeah," Gabriel added. "And we have to learn how to fly that thing."

"**Welcome to the** *Cloud Leopard*!" STEAM exclaimed. "She is a beautiful ship. Yes sir!"

The little robot was waiting outside of the elevator that brought Commander Phillips and the Alpha crew up to the platform that held the spaceship.

"It's bigger than my school," Carly said in awe while gazing up at the behemoth. "It makes me dizzy."

STEAM led the group forward, walking beneath the huge craft, which seemed to stretch overhead forever.

"It takes my breath away to be near something so giant," Piper said.

"It seems impossible," Gabriel said. "Then again, I didn't think robots could walk and talk. No offense, Steamer."

Dash caught movement out of the corner of his eye. It was something small that flashed quickly across the hull far to their right.

"Whoa, what was that?" he exclaimed.

Everyone looked, but whatever it was had disappeared.

"What did it look like?" Piper asked.

"Could have been a bird but it was really hauling," Dash replied.

The question remained unanswered. As they continued on, Dash kept glancing back, hoping to get another glimpse.

"STEAM will give you a brief tour. There's a lot to take in, but trust me, by launch day you'll know this ship inside and out."

"Commander Phillips?" Carly said.

"Yes?"

"For what it's worth, I think you chose the best possible crew."

"I agree," Phillips replied with a rare smile. "Enjoy the tour."

"This way," STEAM called. "Time for you to meet the *Cloud Leopard.*"

The four crew members followed the little robot toward a ramp that led up and into the belly of the ship, near its tail. They walked slowly, taking in every detail of the vehicle as if they were witnessing an impossible dream come true.

Phillips watched as they walked up the ramp and disappeared into the ship.

"Big day," a man said as he approached Phillips.

Phillips turned quickly to see the blond teenager who had been observing the competition from the catwalk above the event arena. He wore a similar dark blue jumpsuit to the one Commander Phillips had on.

"It went well, don't you think?" Phillips asked.

"I do," the young man said. "How did the others take the news?"

"Disappointed, to varying degrees," Phillips replied.

"What was Dash's reaction?"

"Confused," Phillips said.

"Will he accept the risk?"

"I don't know. We should be prepared to go with an alternate."

"Let's hope it won't come to that," the young man said, and the two walked away from the *Cloud Leopard*.

STEAM and the crew stood tight together in a space that was barely large enough to hold all of them.

"This is an air lock," STEAM explained. "In case you need to leave the ship while in space."

"Leave the ship?" Carly said, shaking her head. "That won't be happening."

STEAM continued, "The *Cloud Leopard* will be launched from Earth without a crew on board. Once it is in space, it will not land again. You will travel to and from it aboard a shuttlecraft called the *Cloud Cat.*"

"We have to learn how to fly that too?" Piper asked.

"Yes," STEAM replied. "We will now enter the engine room."

A sliding door opened with the hiss of air and the crew stepped into Wonderland.

"Oh man!" Dash exclaimed.

"Wow" was all Carly could say.

"This just keeps on getting better," Gabriel said in awe.

The space was the size of an auditorium. Directly in front of them sat an array of vehicles, all built from the same silver steel material as the *Cloud Leopard*.

"You will use these vehicles during the mission," STEAM explained. "There is a hovercraft, personal water vehicles, a two-person submarine, and a rover."

The crew went straight to the vehicles, giddy at the idea of playing with the wondrous, oversized toys.

"How cool is this?" Carly said, breathless.

"These are great," Dash said. "But why do we need them? Isn't the mission about going to a planet to dig up some stuff and get back?"

"Yes, but you need to be prepared for anything and everything, yes sir," STEAM said.

"Yeah," Gabriel said. "Don't argue. I want to take these babies out for a drive."

"You will have plenty of time to practice," STEAM said. "Time to move on."

The group re-formed and walked deeper into the compartment. One whole wall was taken up with an array of hard drives with thousands of colorful, winking lights. Beneath the drives were several touch-screen monitors that showed dozens of schematics of the engines and also held the ship's controls.

"We are on the lower deck," STEAM said. "There is another deck above us. The engines are below. All engine functions are controlled and maintained right here."

"We're going to have to learn how to work all this stuff?" Piper asked nervously.

"Yes," STEAM replied. "But mostly as a backup. The ship is automated. Maintenance is performed by the ZRKs."

"The who?" Dash asked.

As if on cue, a small round object the size of a golf ball flew from behind the vehicles and past their heads. Everyone ducked, though they didn't need to, for the sphere had no intention of hitting anyone. It flew toward the rows of monitors and hovered in front of one like a high-tech hummingbird.

"That's what I saw outside!" Dash exclaimed. "It was flying across the hull of the ship."

The sphere was surrounded by multiple small rotors, which gave it lift and propulsion. A small panel on the device opened up and a tiny mechanical arm emerged. It gently tapped the screen to change the setting on one of the sliding controls. The arm retracted and the tiny gizmo flew off.

"Get outta here," Gabriel said, stunned.

"That was a ZRK," STEAM said. "There are too many of them to count, and more are being built all the time. In fact, they build themselves. They keep the ship running smoothly, not to mention many other useful tasks."

"They can think?" Carly asked.

"Not like me, no sir," STEAM said. "They are each programmed to perform a specific function."

"They're kind of cute," Piper said.

"Now this is important," STEAM said, and waddled forward.

He led them to a large metal rectangular device that was built into the hull. It stood eight feet high and ten feet wide. Across the face were seven small doors with windows and one large, oven-like door. Below the doors was a control panel with a rectangular touch screen.

"This is the most essential piece of equipment on board," STEAM explained. "It is the Element Fuser. This is where you will insert the raw elements you retrieve to be processed into the Source. Without this device, your mission means nothing."

"Note to self," Gabriel said. "Take care of the Element Fuser."

"Let us continue," STEAM said.

They walked ahead to the forward wall, where a door slid open that led to a long, narrow corridor.

"This leads to the bow of the ship," STEAM explained. "There is a parallel corridor on the deck above."

On the lower deck, the gym was two stories high and had loads of sports gear like a trampoline, a basketball court, stationary bikes, and an elevated running track.

"What about gravity?" Dash asked. "You can't do much running on a track if you're floating in zero *g*'s."

"The *Cloud Leopard* creates artificial gravity," STEAM replied.

"So far so good," Carly said. "Let's see more."

STEAM led them out of the training center and across the corridor, where another door slid open to reveal a large compartment that was part library, part laboratory. One whole side of the hull had shelves loaded with books. The opposite side had long tables with workstations and computer screens.

"This is the library," STEAM said. "Between paper books and digital files, you will have access to thousands of volumes. I am sorry to say that there is no Internet in space."

"Okay, so maybe the ship's not totally awesome," Gabriel said.

"Why the lab setup?" Piper asked.

"Research," STEAM explained. "In case something you find needs close examination."

"It's perfect," Carly said with enthusiasm.

They moved forward until they reached two doors facing one another on opposite sides of the corridor.

"The door to our right leads to the medical bay," STEAM said. "Piper, Commander Phillips wants to focus your training on being the medic of the crew. Is that something you would like?"

Piper's eyes went wide with excitement.

"Absolutely!" she declared. "That is *exactly* what I'd like to do!"

"This opposite door is off-limits," STEAM said. "It is a safety issue."

"Is that where the fuel is kept?" Piper asked.

"You could say that," STEAM replied. "Now to the upper deck."

An elevator brought them up, and STEAM pointed out the two dorms where they would be sleeping, the recreation room for relaxing, the dining hall, and the galley.

"Do we have to learn to cook?" Carly asked.

"No. That is a ZRK task. They will cook and clean for you."

Gabriel's eyes went wide. "You mean I don't have to clear my place or wash dishes?"

"No sir," STEAM replied.

"Somebody pinch me because I am dreaming!" Gabriel said.

"One last stop," STEAM said. "I am saving the best for last."

At the end of the long corridor, a door slid open and the Alpha crew got their first look at the navigation deck of the *Cloud Leopard.* The first thing they saw was the long, wraparound front window that looked out over the desert. Mounted above it was an eight-foot-wide monitor. Beneath the window were multiple touch screens.

Four flight seats stood next to each other, side by side, facing forward. Each had the exact same touch-pad control on the armrest that the candidates used during their race through the virtual asteroid field.

"This is where you will be whenever the *Cloud Leopard* enters or exits Gamma Speed," STEAM explained.

"Gamma Speed?" Dash asked. "What's that?"

"The technology that will allow you to travel the vast distance to the Source. Without Gamma Speed, the trip would take decades."

Dash's enthusiasm instantly evaporated when he realized that it was Gamma Speed technology that scrambled the metabolism of anyone over the age of fourteen.

"Now," STEAM said, "one last feature."

STEAM waddled to the rear wall of the navigation deck to a large circular hole in the hull. It was three feet in diameter with a horizontal bar above it.

"Have you noticed these?" he asked. "There is also one over there."

He pointed to the opposite side of the navigation deck, where there was an identical hole cut into the same wall.

"I saw them," Carly said. "They're everywhere."

"This portal leads into a series of tubes that are all over the ship. Most you cannot see because they are behind walls and belowdecks."

"What are they for?" Dash asked.

"The *Cloud Leopard* is a very large ship," STEAM said.

"Moving from one compartment to another can be time-consuming. That is why you can choose to fly."

"Fly?" Carly said, confused.

Next to the opening was a panel full of symbols. STEAM touched it, gave the kids a salute, and jumped into the hole. There was a brief sound of rushing air and STEAM was gone.

"Whoa, what?" Gabriel exclaimed, and ran to the portal.

"Where did he go?" Piper cried.

"Right here," STEAM said.

The four kids spun around to see STEAM standing in front of the portal on the opposite side of the navigation deck.

"No way," Carly said, stunned.

"It is a high-speed transportation system," STEAM said. "You can get from the navigation deck to the engine room in eight seconds flat. Want to try?"

"Heck yeah!" Gabriel declared.

STEAM hurried back to the first portal, where Gabriel stood waiting.

"This is a diagram of the ship," he said, referring to the control panel. "Touch the spot that says where you are and slide your finger to where you want to go."

"Like this?" Gabriel asked.

He put his finger on the dot that designated the portal he stood in front of. It lit up green. He slid his finger to the galley, leaving a trail of light that showed his route.

"That is it!" STEAM declared. "Happy landings!"

Gabriel looked into the hole, suddenly unsure.

"Just jump in?" he asked.

"Yes sir," STEAM replied.

Gabriel gave a shrug, grabbed the bar with both hands, and launched himself in feetfirst.

There was the same quick whoosh of air that was quickly drowned out by . . .

"Yeahhhh!"

Gabriel's scream was gone in an instant.

The others stared at the portal, not sure what to do.

"Did it work?" Carly asked.

"Yeah, it worked!" Gabriel announced as he ran back onto the navigation deck from the corridor. "That was awesome! I was like . . . flying on a cushion of air! You guys gotta try!"

"I, uh, I can't," Piper said. "It's not like I can walk when I get to the other side."

STEAM approached Piper and put his small mechanical hand on her arm to offer comfort.

"I am sorry," he said.

"That's okay," Piper said with a shrug. "We can't have big old wheelchairs all over the ship."

"That is true," STEAM said. "But there is something we can do that is even better."

STEAM kept his hand on Piper's arm and touched a few buttons on her Mobile Tech Band. A soft tone sounded and the word INCOMING appeared on her monitor.

"Incoming?" Piper said quizzically. "What's incoming?"

A slight whooshing sound was heard as a silver device floated out of the portal. It was a sleek seat with arms, a backrest, and a curved screen with controls. The device floated there silently. Waiting.

"What is it?" Piper asked, wide-eyed.

"Your new wheelchair," STEAM said. "Though it does not have wheels."

"It's an air chair!" Dash exclaimed.

"For me?" Piper asked, barely able to contain her excitement.

"Four of them will be kept around the ship," STEAM said. "They are more efficient for spaceship maneuvering, yes sir. They can even transition to an upright position."

"That is awesome!" Carly shouted with joy.

Piper drove herself over to the hovering craft. She looked at it with a frown, trying to figure out how to board.

"Just this once," she said. "I'm going to need a little help."

Carly and Dash immediately ran to her, lifted her out of the wheelchair, and deposited her gently into the air chair. The chair dipped a little with her weight, then compensated and floated still. Piper grasped the joystick and gently eased it forward. The chair floated ahead.

"Yeah!" Gabriel shouted.

Piper moved the stick back and the chair floated back. She pushed down and the chair sank to the floor. She lifted it up and the chair rose up again. She moved gently to the right, then to the left.

"Easy?" STEAM asked.

She gave the robot a sly smile and jammed the stick hard to the right. Instantly, she flew into a fast spin.

"Yeah, it's easy!" she screamed with absolute joy.

Everyone laughed and applauded.

"No! Wait!" STEAM cried. "Be careful!"

Piper pulled out of the spin, looking dizzy.

"Wow, won't be doing that again," she said.

She focused and found STEAM.

"C'mere, little man," she said.

STEAM hurried over to her as Piper dropped the chair to the deck. She leaned over and gave the robot a hug.

"Thank you," she said. "It's perfect."

"You are very welcome," STEAM replied.

"I see you've completed the tour," Commander Phillips said as he stepped onto the navigation deck.

Everyone started chattering, all wanting to be heard and give their thoughts about the ship.

"Whoa, whoa, I understand," he said. "It is very impressive. We wanted to make it as comfortable and functional as possible."

"Then mission accomplished," Gabriel said.

"You're going to have plenty of time to explore," Phillips said. "But right now there are media people outside who would like to talk to you."

The kids exchanged uncertain looks.

"I've never been interviewed before," Carly said with concern.

"Just answer their questions as best as you can. STEAM, take them out, please."

"Yes sir!" the robot declared, and walked for the door.

"Whoa, wait, can we take the tube?" Gabriel asked.

"Go for it," Phillips said.

"Race you there," Piper declared, and flew out of the navigation deck at full speed.

"Eeehaaa!" she screamed, her voice echoing through the corridor as she sped away.

Gabriel ran for the tube.

"No way you're beating me!" he shouted as he traced his route, jumped in, and was gone.

"You should try, Carly," STEAM said.

Carly was tentative. She traced the route on the pad and looked to STEAM for verification.

"Perfect," he said. "Do not be afraid."

Carly looked at the tube with trepidation, then suddenly lunged at the bar and grabbed it as if she were doing gymnastics on the uneven bars.

"Let's go!" she screamed, and swung into the tube.

"You next, STEAM," Phillips said. "We'll follow."

"Yes sir," STEAM said. He quickly input the route, then leapt in and disappeared.

Phillips and Dash were left alone.

There was a long moment of awkward silence.

"Time for us to talk," Phillips said.

13

"So am I going to explode just before we get home?" Dash asked.

Commander Phillips took a deep, troubled breath.

"You know how important this mission is," he said. "And you are the perfect choice to lead it."

"So either you're sending me on a suicide mission, or you're not all that sure about this age-metabolism horror-thing."

"Neither," Phillips said. "If you go on this mission and turn fourteen years old out there, you might die. At the very least you will have some physical problems."

"So it *is* suicide."

"No," Phillips said with confidence. "There's another option. Let me ask you a question: Until you heard about Project Alpha, did you imagine any of this could exist?"

Dash said, "I didn't believe it *after* I heard about it either. Not really. I mean, seriously? Deep-space travel. Holograms. Intelligent robots. Gamma Speed. It's all pretty . . . impossible. But then I saw the *Cloud Leopard.*"

"And you're only beginning to learn about the technology we've developed."

"Pretty impressive, except you can't figure out how to keep a kid from growing too old to fly."

Phillips smiled.

That threw Dash. Phillips didn't smile much. He was usually all business.

"We have been developing a biologic," Phillips said. "A cellular treatment if you will. When administered properly, it can slow the aging process."

Dash stared at Phillips, trying to get his brain to make sense of what he had just heard.

"You invented the fountain of youth?" he asked, stunned.

"It's not that dramatic," Phillips said. "The effect is temporary, but we are able to arrest the natural aging process of cells. What I'm saying, Dash, is that if you agree to this treatment, we think we can keep you young enough to fly."

Dash's mind raced. Of all the amazing things he had heard, this may have been the most incredible. He walked to the forward window and looked out at the desert beyond, imagining what the view would be like once the *Cloud Leopard* was in space.

"Why didn't you tell me about this before?" he asked.

"Because I hadn't made the final crew selection," Phillips replied. "And using this treatment obviously isn't the ideal way to go. There are risks."

"Like?"

"The treatment must be administered daily and at specific times. It's a very strict regime. Failing to follow it exactly would erase the benefits and, well, you'd begin to age normally again."

"That would be bad," Dash said.

"Yes, that would be bad."

"What happens after I get back home?"

"You stop the treatments and your cells resume aging naturally again. It would be as though it never happened."

Dash glanced around at the wonders of the navigation deck.

"You waited to tell me until after I saw the ship," Dash said. "You wanted me hooked."

"I wanted you to fully understand our capabilities. You said it yourself. You weren't convinced any of this was real. Now you know it is."

"Yeah, now I know," Dash repeated thoughtfully. "And I'm scared."

"If you choose not to go, I'd understand," Phillips said. "You'll be on a plane back to Florida by nightfall."

"Who would replace me?"

"I don't know. They're all capable but you're the one who gives us the best chance of success. That's why I'm making this offer. I understand it's a tough decision. Maybe we should call your mother and get her opinion."

"No!" Dash said quickly. "I know what she'll say and you won't want to hear it. I have to make the decision myself."

"And that's exactly why I chose you," Phillips said. "It's all right to be scared, but a leader can never be afraid to make tough choices. Can you make the tough choice, Dash?"

The bus carrying Anna, Ravi, Siena, and Niko drove quickly along the desolate desert highway, headed for the international airport outside of Las Vegas. There were no Humvees to escort them and no heavily armed helicopters in the sky to guide them safely on their way. Their job was complete. Security was no longer an issue.

Or so they thought.

High above, an unmarked military helicopter trailed them.

Nobody on the bus knew. Nobody saw. They were too far out in the Mojave Desert for anyone to take notice. There wasn't another car within fifty miles.

The helicopter swooped low, matching the speed of the bus. It dropped quickly, square in the blind spot of the driver. It approached the bus from behind at a forty-five degree angle until it was thirty feet above it. The side door of the chopper slid open, and with a burst of speed, the helicopter flew forward until it was directly over the bus. A rope was dropped and a dark figure slid down it quickly. Three seconds later, the figure landed on top of the bus. The figure released the rope and the helicopter flew off.

The dark figure was a commando. A professional. He wore a black hood with a mask over his face that had two metallic disks near the mouth. He quickly pulled a pack off his back and reached inside to retrieve a canister that looked like a small fire extinguisher. Protruding from one end was a long, needlelike shaft. The commando grasped the canister, raised it high, and brought it down hard. The needle pierced the skin of the bus's roof and the commando opened a valve at the canister's base.

He moved quickly, catlike, headed for the front of the bus. As he ran he pulled a long metal tool from his belt. He reached the front and leaned over the right side, jamming the tool into the top of the door. With a violent thrust, he forced the door open. Like an acrobat, he grasped the top of the door frame and flipped himself over the side . . .

. . . to land inside the bus.

He went straight for the driver, who was slumped over,

unconscious. The commando quickly released the seat belt and yanked the driver out and onto the floor. The commando took control of the bus and shot a quick look to the rear to confirm that all four passengers were also unconscious.

He reached for a walkie-talkie that was clipped to his chest.

"The babies are asleep," he said through the filters attached to his mask. "I'm behind the wheel and headed for home."

Two miles ahead was the intersection of two highways. Going north would lead straight to the international airport.

The commando went south.

Carly, Gabriel, and Piper sat behind a table full of microphones, fielding questions from the dozens of reporters who crowded around the stage.

"Do you miss your families?" one reporter asked.

"Sure," Carly replied. "But we talk to them most every night. I get to tell them exactly how my day went."

"Piper," another reporter called out. "How do you think your disability is going to affect the mission?"

All eyes went to the small blond girl in the chair.

The flying chair.

Piper eased the chair back away from the table. She floated slowly around to the front of the stage, then throttled up and flew over the heads of the reporters. They all ducked, laughing. Piper flew back to the stage and settled into her place behind the table.

"What disability are you talking about?" she asked innocently.

The reporters laughed and whistled their approval.

As the cheering continued, Dash stepped up onto the stage.

He walked behind the others and headed for the empty seat that was reserved for him.

"Everything okay?" Carly whispered.

Dash nodded and sat in his spot.

"Dash!" one of the reporters called out. "Congratulations on being named commander of the Voyagers. Just one question: Are you scared?"

Dash looked at the others, who stared at him expectantly. He cleared his throat and said, "Sure. Who wouldn't be? But I'm not going to let that stop us. None of us are."

The Alpha crew broke out in wide, confident grins.

Anna slowly opened her eyes. Her head hurt. Why did her head hurt? She gradually woke up to focus and looked around to see she was still on the bus, only the bus wasn't moving.

"Hey," she called out to the others, who were still sleeping. "Wake up."

The others roused slowly, with similar headaches.

"Are we there?" Niko asked.

"We're somewhere," Ravi said while looking out of the window. "But it's not the airport."

They were still in the desert. The bus was parked on a desolate unpaved road.

"Where's the driver?" Niko asked.

Nobody had the answer.

"Interesting," Siena said. "Any theories on who those two people might be?"

They all crowded around Siena to look out of the side window.

Parked several yards away was the helicopter with no

identifying markings. Standing in front of it, shoulder to shoulder, were two commandos dressed in black.

The door to the bus opened and a third man entered. He was an older man with a shock of silver gray hair and intense dark eyes. They had never seen him before—but he had been observing them since they arrived at Base Ten. He walked slowly up the aisle with a smile that was meant to put them at ease but seemed more forced than friendly.

Everyone huddled together for security.

The man stopped, looked at each in turn as if taking attendance, and clapped.

"Bravo," he said. "I am so proud to meet you all."

The kids exchanged confused looks.

"Who are you?" Anna asked tentatively.

"I'm the man who is going to give you a second chance," he said. "If you're smart enough to take it."

14

It was the night before launch.

After a year of hard work to get on the team, and another six months of training, it was almost time to go.

T-minus twelve hours and counting.

Dash, Carly, Gabriel, and Piper were eating dinner silently in the dorm at Base Ten. It wasn't until they'd all finished and pushed their trays away that Carly said what was on everybody's mind.

"Are we ready?" she asked. "I mean really ready? Sure, we can fly the simulators and run the systems, but this is for real now. I mean, we're going into space."

"I think we're ready," Dash said confidently. "This mission is too important for them to send us if we weren't."

"But what happens if we run into things they didn't count on?" Carly asked. "There's no way we've been trained for every possibility."

"That's when we earn our ten million bucks," Gabriel said.

During the hours and weeks of simulator training, Gabriel had established himself as the best aviator of the crew and was named the official pilot and navigator. He had the uncanny ability to think three steps ahead and fly safely through every challenge thrown at him.

"It would be nice to know exactly where we are going," Piper added, bringing up a point they had been speculating about for weeks.

"Seriously," Carly said. "I mean, we launch tomorrow!"

Carly was assigned to be the ship's science and technology officer. She'd spent months learning every detail of the ship while honing various skills like troubleshooting the Element Fuser and analyzing the density of a celestial storm.

Piper had trained to be the crew's medic. Much of her training was in the medical bay of the *Cloud Leopard,* performing simulated medical emergencies and learning how to access the vast medical database.

"Try not to stress," Dash said. "Failure is not an option, right?"

"Let's hope not," Carly said nervously.

As commander of the mission, Dash had to learn it all. He not only had to be prepared to make decisions based on his crew's recommendations, but he also had to be ready and able to fill in for any one of them.

In addition to their training, they did their best to make the *Cloud Leopard* their home. They'd worked out in the gym and watched movies in the recreation room. They'd decorated their quarters and made daily video-calls to their families. As the weeks stretched into months, the crew had grown more sure of their skills, and more trusting of each other.

"We're going to do this and we're going to get back with the Source," Dash said. "I have total confidence."

"Good," Phillips said as he stepped into the room with STEAM right behind him. "I do too." He stood at the end of the table. "Big day tomorrow. I want you all to get a good night's sleep."

"I doubt I'll sleep at all," Carly said, grumbling.

"Is that because of nerves?" Phillips asked. "Or something else?"

Dash stood up to represent the group.

"We've done everything you've asked us to do," he began. "We left our families. We worked hard. We studied like crazy. We agreed to fly to the other side of the universe. We've done it all, gladly, because it's important."

"One hundred percent correct," Phillips said. "Where is this going?"

"That's the question," Dash shot back. "Where is this going? Where are *we* going? We're supposed to launch tomorrow, but we're as clueless about what comes next as the day we got here."

"We deserve to know where we're going, Commander," Piper said. "We earned it."

Phillips gave a tired sigh, and for the first time the crew realized that he had been working as hard as they had.

"We've been overloading you with information," Phillips said. "My concern is that it's too much to handle, even for exceptional minds like yours. I didn't want to look too far ahead and have things slip through the cracks right in front of us. That's why I've been holding back on giving you all the information about your flight." Phillips took a breath. "But you're right," he said with conviction. "It's time you learned. Come with me."

Everyone followed Phillips out of the dining hall and into the rec room. The commander strode to the large monitor that hung from the wall on one end, while the crew took the comfortable seats facing it.

He pointed a remote control and the monitor flashed to life with a detailed, three-dimensional star map.

"Your destination is a planet that was discovered by a deep-space probe nearly twenty years ago."

The image on screen zoomed in, flashing past thousands upon thousands of stars, creating a dizzying journey into deep space. The image eventually slowed until a single green planet filled the screen.

"It's called J-16. Its atmosphere and gravity are similar to Earth's. We're not entirely sure of the extent of life there."

"But things do live there?" Carly asked.

"Yes, but we don't believe it is intelligent life as we know it here on Earth."

Carly diligently input notes on her Mobile Tech Band.

"And what exactly are we looking for?" Dash asked.

"One step at a time, remember?" Phillips said. "Let's get you there first."

"Okay, what about the first step?" Gabriel said. "Do I plot a course through the galaxy?"

"No," Phillips said. "The *Cloud Leopard* is pre-programmed to make the journey. Once you leave orbit you'll jump into Gamma Speed. The trip will take fifteen days."

"At that speed we're going to be pretty far from home," Dash said.

"Yes," Phillips said. "But you won't be alone. I'll be in constant contact."

VOYAGERS
TOP-SECRET MISSION BRIEF
RAVI CHAVAN
COUNTRY OF ORIGIN India (Mumbai)
PRIMARY SKILLS / NOTES
Technology, software/hardware development
DASH CONROY
COUNTRY OF ORIGIN USA (Florida)
PRIMARY SKILLS / NOTES
Team leadership, problem solving
CARLY DIAMOND
COUNTRY OF ORIGIN Japan (Tokyo)
PRIMARY SKILLS / NOTES
Languages, analytical skills
SIENA MORETTI
COUNTRY OF ORIGIN Italy (Florence)
PRIMARY SKILLS / NOTES
Command support, research
GABRIEL PARKER
COUNTRY OF ORIGIN USA (Illinois)
PRIMARY SKILLS / NOTES
Navigation, meteorology
NIKO RODRIGUEZ
COUNTRY OF ORIGIN Brazil (São Paulo)
PRIMARY SKILLS / NOTES
Medicine, emergency surgery
PROJECT ALPHA
FINALISTS
ANNA TURNER
COUNTRY OF ORIGIN USA (Michigan)
PRIMARY SKILLS / NOTES
Leadership, deductive reasoning
PIPER WILLIAMS
COUNTRY OF ORIGIN USA (California)
PRIMARY SKILLS / NOTES
Medicine, surgery, pharmacology

ZRK PROBE DATA | PLANET J-16

VOYAGERS

TOP-SECRET MISSION BRIEF

PROJECT ALPHA

CONFIDENTIAL

SECURITY UPDATE

To ensure the success of Project Alpha, all staff members and operatives are ordered not to discuss mission details with *anyone* outside their direct chain of command.

This includes *all Cloud Leopard* crew members.

Effective immediately:
ANY and ALL information regarding mission details will be disseminated on a NEED-TO-KNOW BASIS ONLY.

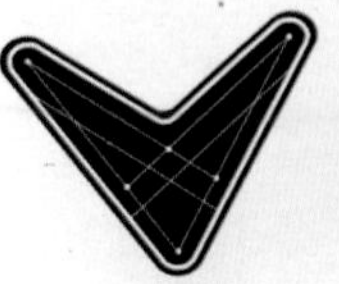

1000
500
9200
9800
10000
TOPOGRAPHY DATA
PLANET J-16 / SECTOR 439–445
Proposed *Cloud Cat* landing area.
0.66
14.8
9600
DANGER
PLANET J-16 - Unidentified living organism. Highly aggressive. Approach with extreme caution.
8800

ZRK PROBE DATA | PLANET J-16

"That's nice," Carly said. "But checking in from Earth isn't the same as having your life on the line a million miles from home."

"I know that," Phillips said. "That's why I'm sending along a fifth crew member."

The group broke out with a jumble of shouts of surprise. Phillips raised his hands to quiet them down.

"Who is it?" Gabriel asked.

"Me," STEAM said.

All eyes shot to the little robot.

"You did not think I would miss the fun, did you? No sir!"

The group erupted again, this time with cries of joy.

"All right, Steamer!" said Piper.

"STEAM knows everything about the ship's systems," Phillips said. "He will guide you through each phase of the mission.

"But you're right," he continued. "Surprises will happen. It's inevitable. To deal with the unknown, we need you all up there. People who think. Who adapt. Who have intuition. Picking you four wasn't just about finding out who could best pilot a ship; it was about putting together a crew who can think on their feet."

The weight of Phillips's words rested heavily on them.

"Failure is not an option. Right?" Dash said.

"Not if we want to keep the world spinning," Phillips replied. "Are we good?"

Everyone nodded numbly.

"Good. You are one hundred percent prepared for this, trust me. Tomorrow, you go to space. For tonight, try to get some rest."

Everyone got up to head out.

“Dash, wait a minute?” Phillips said.

“What’s up?” Dash asked as the others filed out.

Phillips placed a black metallic briefcase on the table and opened it to reveal an array of what looked like white pens.

“Time to get started,” Phillips said.

Dash’s face dropped. He knew exactly what Phillips meant.

“This is the stuff?” he asked.

“Each of these vials contains a single dose,” Phillips explained. “It’s simple to use. Flip off the cap to reveal the injector, then jab it anywhere on your body. Your thigh is an easy spot. You can even do it through your clothes. You’ll barely feel it.”

Dash lifted one of the doses and examined it closely.

“What’s the schedule?” he asked.

“The injection must be given every day within twenty-four hours of the last. It wouldn’t be the end of the world if you didn’t hit the window exactly, but if you miss a dose entirely—”

“Then that would be the end of the world,” Dash said. “At least for me.”

Phillips didn’t respond.

“I don’t want the other guys to know,” Dash said as he stared at the injector. “They’re stressed enough.”

“I understand,” Phillips said. “But STEAM knows. You have to have backup.”

Dash took a deep breath, blew it out, and said, “All right then, happy unbirthday to me.”

He lifted the injector, flipped the cap off, and jabbed it into his leg. With a slight click, the first dose was done.

“And my clock is stopped,” Dash said. “I hope you guys know what you’re doing.”

None of the crew slept much that night. There were too many thoughts bouncing around in their heads. They had all made one last video-call with their families. It would be a full year before they would see them again, and the last good-byes were difficult.

The preparation was done. The training was complete. There was nothing left to do but watch the clock tick down to zero.

"Dash?" Gabriel said quietly, sometime after midnight.

"I'm awake," Dash said.

"Something's really bothering me."

"We're ready, Gabe," Dash assured him.

"I know."

"Then what?"

"What if we blow it? I mean, what if we just flat-out fail and don't bring the Source back? The whole world is counting on us. How could we face anybody again?"

Dash thought for a moment and then said, "There are two answers to that. Like Phillips said, all we can do is take it one step at a time. Don't think of the big picture; it's overwhelming. Just worry about the next step."

"What's the other answer?" Gabriel asked.

"I take it back," Dash said. "There is no other answer. Failure is not an option."

15

Before sunrise the next morning, hundreds of Base Ten personnel were gathered near the hangar that held the launch platform for the *Cloud Leopard.* All eyes were on the mighty silver spaceship as it lifted off slowly from the launch platform. With an intense burst of power it shot straight up, impossibly fast. The ground rocked with a single violent shudder that came from the immense force expelled from the ship's engines. There was no trail of smoke, just the rapidly shrinking image of a giant ship speeding faster than any man-made object of that size had ever moved.

The cheers from the crowd were deafening as the ship became a small black dot that quickly disappeared.

Dash, Carly, Gabriel, and Piper stood apart from the others, set off by their slick new navy jumpsuits with holographic V-shaped emblems. They had been surprisingly chipper all morning. They talked sports. They told dumb jokes. They tried to talk about anything and everything except the mission. But when the *Cloud Leopard* started counting down, they fell silent, and they hadn't spoken a word all through liftoff.

"Check your MTBs," STEAM instructed.

All four looked to their Mobile Tech Bands to see six simple words: THE CLOUD LEOPARD IS IN ORBIT!

The crowd continued cheering.

"I guess that means we're next," Carly said.

Commander Phillips approached, and Dash stepped forward.

"Alpha crew reporting for duty," Dash said.

Phillips smiled warmly and led them to the elevator that brought them up to the launch platform. Now that the *Cloud Leopard* was gone, the much smaller *Cloud Cat* sat alone in the center of the vast platform. It was about the size of a small house. They walked up the ramp and into the shuttle with STEAM leading the way.

"Perfect day to fly. Yes sir!" the robot said cheerily.

"I'm glad you're here, STEAM," Piper said.

The interior of the *Cloud Cat* was large enough for four flight seats, two forward and two behind, with enough room to walk between them. Gabriel took the front left pilot's seat. Dash settled in next to him. Carly sat behind Gabriel, while Piper transferred from her air chair to the rear right. STEAM secured himself against the hull behind them with nylon straps.

Phillips checked every last strap, making sure the crew was secure.

"I won't say good-bye," Phillips said. "We'll be talking to each other constantly. I also won't say good luck because you won't need it. You're all too good."

"So what *will* you say?" Gabriel asked.

Phillips thought for a moment, and coughed as if fighting back emotions. "I want you to know that I'm proud of you all and I wish I was going with you."

"Thanks, Commander," Dash said. "See you soon."

Phillips nodded and exited the shuttle before anyone could see how choked up he was.

The four crew members were alone. They exchanged nervous looks.

"I guess this is it," Dash said. "Final words?"

"Yeah," Gabriel said. "Don't say final. We're just getting started."

"Fair enough," Dash said. "Let's fly. You're on, Gabe."

Gabriel put on his dark flight glasses, then hit the switch that lifted the ramp up into the ship and sealed the hatch. Nothing was out of the ordinary, except that this was not a training exercise.

"Alpha Control," Gabriel said in his most professional pilot voice. "This is *Cloud Cat.* We are secure and ready to launch."

"Roger, *Cloud Cat,*" the Alpha Control voice said back to them. "Initiating launch sequence."

Gabriel took his hands off the controls and sat back.

"Okay, kids," he said. "Nothing to do but enjoy the ride."

Alpha Control announced, "*Cloud Cat,* you are go for launch. Thrusters will engage in five . . . four . . . three . . . two . . . one . . . engage."

The ship shuddered as the engines sprang to life. Everyone was pushed gently into their seats as the craft lifted slowly off the deck.

"Liftoff," Alpha Control announced. "Ten seconds until main boosters."

"My mouth is too dry to swallow," Piper said.

"No problem," Dash said calmly. "We've done this a thousand times."

"Yeah," Carly said. "Except for the leaving Earth part."

". . . three . . . two . . . one . . . engage. Godspeed, Voyagers."

The main boosters kicked in. The increased g-forces pushed everyone deep into their seats as the *Cloud Cat* accelerated rapidly and shot skyward.

On the ground, there were cheers and tears.

In front of their TVs at home, four families watched their children disappear into the heavens.

The *Cloud Cat* gained speed as it fought to break free of Earth's gravity.

"Everybody okay?" Dash asked.

"Good."

"Fine."

"Super fine."

Nothing was out of the ordinary, right down to the sky darkening outside of the forward window port. The crew had seen this all during simulations.

"I have to keep reminding myself this is real," Carly said.

The ship began shaking as it battled the pull of gravity.

"Whoa," Piper said. "This is different."

"Alpha Control," Gabriel said. "This buffeting is more intense than in training. My teeth are chattering."

"You're fine," Alpha Control said. "That's expected."

"Not by me it wasn't," Gabriel replied. "I can't see straight."

The buffeting grew more intense.

Nobody admitted it, but it made them more than nervous.

"Almost done," STEAM declared.

The shaking grew more intense; the crew was pushed further into their seats; and then without a warning the ride smoothed out.

"Well," Gabriel said, relieved. "That was . . . different."

"Look at this!" Piper declared.

She had been clutching a tiny stuffed elephant for good luck. The toy was now floating in front of her. "We're in orbit!"

"Houston," Gabriel said with glee. "We have *no* problem!"

"Say again, *Cloud Cat,*" Alpha Control replied.

"We've achieved orbit," Gabriel answered, more business-like.

The automatic program that would bring the *Cloud Cat* to the *Cloud Leopard* made a course correction and sent the small shuttle on its way. Everyone gazed in wonder out of the forward window at the void of space and the multitude of stars.

"It's just like the simulations," Carly said. "But man, it's *real*!"

"Look at that," Dash declared, pointing to the far side of the forward window.

All eyes went there to see the curve of planet Earth. The deep blue sea was a strong contrast to the dark continents. Strings of white clouds drifted over the California coast like pale cotton candy.

"I wonder how many people down there are thinking about us," Carly asked.

Nobody ventured a guess. The concept was too staggering.

"Fifteen minutes until rendezvous with the *Cloud Leopard,*" Alpha Control announced.

A tiny, silver speck appeared in the distance. It was the *Cloud Leopard,* exactly where it was supposed to be.

"Hey, Steamer," Gabriel said. "How about I turn off the computer and bring us in myself?"

"No sir," STEAM said. "Not a good idea."

"C'mon!" Gabriel cajoled. "Then all that training will be for nothing."

"Better not," STEAM said.

"What do you think, Dash?" Gabriel said. "You're the commander. Can I go for it?"

Dash was torn. He didn't want any problems, but he also wanted to show confidence in the crew. He glanced back to Carly and Piper.

"Okay with me," Carly said with a shrug.

"Go for it," Piper added. "It's not like we haven't done it a few thousand times."

Gabriel gave Dash a big, innocent, pleading smile.

"Okay," Dash said. "Just take it easy."

"Yeah!" Gabriel exclaimed. He pushed his flight glasses firmly onto his nose and placed his hand on the control pad.

"Cloud Cat," Alpha Control immediately said. "You are in manual mode."

"Yes, we are," Gabriel replied. "Just trying to get the feel of this thing."

"I've got a bad feeling about this," STEAM said.

Gabriel focused on the growing spot in space that was the *Cloud Leopard* and increased the thrust to speed up the rendezvous.

"This is way easier than the simulator," Gabriel said.

He put on even more speed. The *Cloud Leopard* took shape. The docking door was open and waiting.

"*Cloud Cat,* reengage computer control," Alpha Control commanded.

"I got this," Gabriel replied.

The *Cloud Leopard* loomed larger.

"We're coming in too fast," Dash warned.

"I've come in way faster than this before," Gabriel shot back.

"Not when we were actually moving," Dash said. "Go back to computer control."

"Relax, I got it," Gabriel said.

The *Cloud Cat* drifted to the right, moving off the center line for approach.

"Reengage the computer, Gabe," Dash said, the strain showing in his voice.

"Almost there," Gabriel said, squinting in concentration.

"Reengage!" Dash shouted. "That's an order!"

Gabriel ignored him. He was too focused on bringing the ship in.

Dash didn't have the reengage control in front of him. Only the pilot did. But Dash had his own pair of flight glasses.

"I'm taking over," he announced, and put on the glasses.

"No!" Gabriel shouted.

Putting on the glasses transferred control of the *Cloud Cat* to Dash, the commander. He put his hand on the control pad and the *Cloud Cat* immediately slowed. Dash brought the ship back to the center line and gently eased it through the docking door.

"Reengaging computer," Gabriel declared, all business.

He punched the control that brought the computer back online and the *Cloud Cat* eased gently into the launch bay. The vehicle settled onto the deck and the engines wound down.

"Alpha Control, we have arrived at the *Cloud Leopard*," Gabriel said.

"Roger, *Cloud Cat,*" Alpha Control replied. "Welcome aboard."

Nobody said anything for several seconds as the launch doors of the *Cloud Leopard* closed. The moment the doors were sealed, the effect of the artificial gravity took over and the crew once again felt the weight of their bodies.

"I had it," Gabriel said angrily to Dash.

"You were going too fast and you were off course," Dash said.

"And what was with the 'that's an order' thing?" Gabriel asked, barely hiding his disdain.

"I'm the commander," Dash said. "And we were in trouble."

"We weren't," Gabriel argued.

"It was a dumb thing to do," Dash said. "Totally unnecessary."

"Whatever," Gabriel shot back. "Next time leave the flying to me, *Commander.*"

Carly leaned in between the two of them and said, "Can we go now?"

The guys turned away from one another and unstrapped. Piper was already in her air chair and STEAM dropped the ramp for them to step off.

"Well," STEAM said. "That was excitement we did not need."

Gabriel stormed off and the others followed. As they rounded to the front of the *Cloud Cat,* several blue ZRKs flew in to inspect the vehicle for damages. The crew ignored them and strode straight for the elevator. Moments later, they were on the upper deck.

Gabriel was angry. Dash was too. The girls were upset as well. What had started out as the adventure of a lifetime had quickly turned into a family squabble.

STEAM led the group forward until they reached the doors to the navigation deck. He turned back to the others and said, "There is something very important that you must remember."

"Really?" Gabriel said, annoyed. "What's that?"

"We are in space. Yes sir!"

The door opened onto the flight deck to reveal a panoramic view of space through the forward window of the *Cloud Leopard.*

The kids were still speechless, but for a very different reason. Up until that moment, the only view they had ever seen through that window was of the desert. Now they were greeted by the infinite beauty of the universe.

"I, uh, I . . . wow" was all Gabriel could say.

The giant monitor above the window came to life with a live image of Commander Phillips.

"What happened?" he demanded, peeved.

"A miscommunication," Dash said quickly. "I thought we were off course, so I authorized manual control. My fault."

Gabriel shot Dash a surprised look.

"It was a mistake," Gabriel said, genuinely sorry. "It won't happen again."

"It can't happen again," Phillips said sternly. "Do you understand?"

"Yes," Dash and Gabriel said at the same time.

"All right, then," Phillips said, calming down. "Let's start again. How does it feel to be in space?"

"Amazing!" Piper said with enthusiasm. "The Earth is beautiful. And the stars . . . there are like . . . billions!"

"What happens now?" Dash asked. "We stay in orbit for a while? Make sure the ship is secure? Settle in to our quarters?"

"Uh, no," Phillips said. "Look at your MTBs."

Everyone raised their arms to see that yet another countdown was in progress. The count moved below five minutes.

"What happens in five minutes?" Carly asked.

"Strap in to your flight seats," Phillips said. "When the count reaches zero, the ship will be in position to break out of orbit and hit the proper trajectory for J-16."

"Whoa," Gabriel said. "You mean we're heading for deep space now? Right now?"

"We could wait until the next orbit but what's the point? Let's get this show on the road."

The crew dove for the seats. Gabriel was in the far left seat. The pilot's seat. Carly was to his immediate right. Piper slid into the next seat over and Dash's seat was on the far right end.

Gabriel put on his pilot's glasses.

"This will be a new experience for you," Phillips said. "The jump to Gamma Speed will be a jolt followed by a smooth ride. This is a programmed event. There will be no need for Gabriel to take manual control. Is that understood?"

All eyes went to Gabriel.

He saw that he was being stared at and said, "I get it! I won't touch a thing."

"One minute," Phillips announced. "How is everyone feeling?"

"Ready," Dash announced.

"Excited," Piper replied.

"Anxious," Carly said.

"All of the above," Gabriel said.

"In fifteen days, the *Cloud Leopard* will arrive and be inserted into orbit around the planet J-16," Phillips said. "From now until then, you will be prepped on how to retrieve the element needed for the Source."

"One step at a time," Dash said.

"Thirty seconds," STEAM announced.

"I envy you all," Phillips said. "You are the first humans to be traveling at Gamma Speed."

"Wait, what?" Carly said. "I thought you said this was all tested."

"Safe journey," Phillips said. "I'll be in touch."

The screen winked out and was replaced by the countdown.

8 . . . 7 . . . 6 . . .

"Should we be worried?" Piper asked nervously.

"Too late now," Dash replied.

. . . 3 . . . 2 . . . 1 . . . IGNITION.

The kids were thrown back into their seats as the *Cloud Leopard* jumped from Earth's orbit, pulled away from the planet's gravity, and entered the state of Gamma Speed.

Next stop, the far side of the universe.

PART TWO

J-16

The heavy sensation from the sudden and dramatic acceleration lasted only a few seconds. After that, the ship settled in and there was barely any sense of movement at all.

"That's it?" Carly asked. "Are we really in Gamma Speed?"

Gabriel touched his control panel and a map of the universe appeared. The *Cloud Leopard* was represented by a small green *A* that stood out brilliantly against the black void and brilliant white stars. The image was moving, though slowly.

"We're on our way," Gabriel declared. "I don't know whether to be freaked out or disappointed. It doesn't even feel like we're going anywhere."

"That's a good thing," Dash said while unbuckling his straps. "I wouldn't want to be bracing myself like that for two weeks."

STEAM joined the group and said, "It is now my job to brief you on the next phase of the mission."

"Finally!" Gabriel declared.

On the monitor, an image of the green planet J-16 appeared.

"An unmanned probe was sent into space years ago,"

STEAM explained. "It sent back these images. The planet is primitive, like Earth a million years ago. This video is from the probe as it made its landing."

The screen changed to a moving shot flying over a dense green tropical jungle. The probe's camera captured images from below as it flashed over a thick canopy that could have been a rain forest in Brazil.

"Atmosphere is breathable; gravity is like Earth," STEAM said.

The probe zipped over the top of the dense canopy, then swooped down low, passing by tall, swaying bushes with leaves the size of blankets. It descended low over a tangle of vines and masses of colorful flowers.

"Where am I supposed to land in that mess?" Gabriel asked.

"Stand by," STEAM said.

The thick ground cover gave way to a wide, grassy meadow that sat in a valley surrounded by distant, towering mountain ranges. Multiple waterfalls cascaded from the cliffs, completing the image of a tropical paradise.

The image showed that the probe descended quickly and landed softly in the grass.

"That is where you land," STEAM said. "Navigation will lock onto the signal from the probe and guide you in, yes sir."

"What kind of life is there?" Carly asked. "Besides all the vegetables."

"Uncertain," STEAM answered. "One thing we know is that there is no intelligent life. At least not as we know it."

"I'll bet there are snakes," Gabriel said. "It looks like the kind of place that has lots of snakes. I hate snakes."

"All the information you will need is stored in our data banks. We have two weeks to prepare," STEAM said.

"All right, then," Dash said. "Welcome home, everybody."

The crew took time to make themselves get used to life aboard the *Cloud Leopard.* Many of their waking hours were spent in the recreation room watching movies and playing games. They worked out in the gym and raced each other through the tubes.

Meals were always a highlight. They ordered from an electronic menu, and soon after, the ZRKs would fly into the dining hall and deliver their food. When the meal was finished, the ZRKs would clear the table and clean up until not a single crumb was left.

The ZRKs were a constant presence. They not only maintained the complex systems of the ship, but they cooked meals, made the bunks, and did the laundry.

"I'm bringing some of these little guys home with me," Gabriel would say multiple times a day.

The journey wasn't all fun. Gabriel constantly checked the progress of the *Cloud Leopard* against the set course. He also continued his flight training in a simulator. The plan was to use the hovercraft to move over the surface of J-16, so he spent much of his time getting used to handling that vehicle.

Piper did daily medical checks on the crew, taking vital signs like temperature and blood pressure. She even did vision and hearing checks. The data was entered and sent back to Base Ten so doctors could monitor the health of the crew.

Carly needed to know the Element Fuser inside and out so she could prepare the Source when the time came. She took items from all over the ship like sugar, water, lint, food scraps . . . anything she could find to practice with the device and see what strange new compounds she could create. Mostly she came up with gook, but it made her confident that she had mastered the machine.

Dash spent a lot of time in the simulators as well.

Gabriel wasn't happy about that. "I don't care if he's the commander," he confided in Carly after a few days. "It's not his job to fly. And he's been monkeying with the Element Fuser and checking up on Piper too. It's like he doesn't trust us to do our jobs."

"He's just trying to stay on top of things," Carly said, attempting to calm him down.

"Yeah, well, if he's so good, maybe Phillips should have sent Dash out here by himself," Gabriel said.

The tension between Dash and Gabriel wouldn't go away, but it was minor compared to the dramatic events that took place only a few days into the flight.

Dash was on the track, running laps. As he finished his daily run, his eye caught a flash of movement in the gym below. It was too big to have been a ZRK, and too small to be one of the crew.

"Hey!" he called. "STEAM? That you?"

No answer.

A shadow moved underneath the trampoline.

"Gabe?" he called but got no reply.

Dash quickly went to the circular stairs that led from the raised track down to the gym floor.

"I know you're there," he called. "I saw you."

Dash moved slowly, cautiously toward the trampoline. His

pulse raced. What was going on? Why wasn't the person answering?

"Stop messing, all right? This isn't funny."

Dash couldn't see beneath the trampoline because his view was blocked by two large exercise balls.

"I know it's you, Gabe. You're going to jump out at me, right?"

Dash got close enough to the balls to touch them.

"All right," he said. "Enough."

He shoved the two balls aside to reveal . . .

. . . a golden retriever.

Dash was so shocked, he couldn't move.

The dog walked up to him, sat down, and lifted his paw to shake.

Dash took it numbly.

"What the heck?" was all he managed to say.

The golden retriever pulled away from him and trotted for the door.

Dash fought to get his wits back and took off after the dog.

"Hey! Stop! Heel! Sit!"

The animal kept moving and ran forward through the corridor.

Dash was right behind him. It was a mistake. It had to be. The dog must have somehow got aboard without anybody knowing.

The dog ran up to the door that led to the room that was off-limits to the crew. He stood with his nose against the door and scratched at it.

"You can't go in there," Dash said. "It's dangerous and . . ."

The door slid open.

Dash's words caught in his throat when he saw who had opened it. Standing inside the off-limits room was yet another unexpected visitor.

It was the blond young man who had been watching the competition from the catwalk on Base Ten.

"You!" Dash exclaimed.

"I see you've met Rocket," the teenager said.

"Rocket?" Dash repeated, stunned.

"My dog."

"And who are you!" Dash demanded.

"My name is Chris. I'll be joining you on your voyage."

17

"What the heck, Commander Phillips!" Gabriel shouted angrily at the monitor as he paced the navigation deck. "Who is this guy?"

The whole crew was there along with STEAM. Chris stood to the side with his hands folded in front. Rocket lay at his feet, dozing.

"Chris is the reason we're all here," Phillips said. "He discovered the Source. He created the Gamma drive. He designed the *Cloud Leopard.* This has been his project from the get-go. I've only been the manager who helped him put it all together."

All four kids turned and looked at Chris with curiosity.

"He looks like he's in high school!" Carly declared. "How is that possible?"

"He's older than he looks," Phillips replied.

"So you're some kind of uber-genius?" Dash asked.

"I am," Chris said matter-of-factly. "And this is my dog, Rocket."

Rocket raised his head and wagged his tail.

"Why didn't you tell us?" Piper asked.

"Seriously," Gabriel said. "We said no more lies and this is a whopper."

"I didn't lie," Phillips said. "I simply didn't tell you everything."

"That's for sure," Dash said. "This one step at a time thing is getting old."

"You weren't told for security purposes," Phillips said. "Project Alpha has been top secret for years. *Chris* has been top secret. The information he holds and the technology he invented is priceless. Now that the mission is public, there are those who would do anything to get hold of him. We simply couldn't risk that."

Piper flew to STEAM and said, "You told us the off-limits room had the fuel to power the *Cloud Leopard.*"

"It does," STEAM said. "That is Chris's room. Without him, there is no Alpha Project. He is the fuel. Yes sir."

"Wait," Dash said. "I thought adults couldn't survive Gamma Speed?"

"I have been working with the Gamma model for years," Chris said. "I devised a serum that will allow me to withstand the shock of a Gamma jump, as you can see. But it is specific to my physiology. It would not be effective with anyone else." He smiled sheepishly, then continued, "Well, Rocket also has special treats."

Dash stared straight into Chris's eyes, trying to read his thoughts. Did Chris know that he was taking a daily dose to prevent aging?

"Unbelievable" was all Dash said.

"What else is there, Phillips?" Gabriel demanded. "What haven't you told us? It's okay. You can be honest. We're stuck.

We can't turn back. We're on our way and we still don't even know what we're looking for."

Phillips looked at Chris and said, "It's time they knew it all."

"Darn right it is!" Carly said.

"But I don't want to hear it from Commander Phillips," Dash said. "If Chris is the brains, it has to come from him."

All eyes went to Chris.

Chris gave Rocket a pat on the head and walked calmly forward to stand under the monitor. When he spoke, it was with the precision of a computer.

"We are headed to planet J-16 where we will retrieve one of the elements that will be combined to create the Source," Chris said.

"*One* of the elements?" Piper said. "There's more than one?"

"There are six," Chris replied. "That is the purpose of the Element Fuser. We must gather all six elements in order to create the compound I have named the Source."

"So we have to find six elements on J-16?" Dash asked.

"No. Only one of the elements is native to that world. Once it has been retrieved, we must then journey to five other planets. That is why, as you know, this mission will last an entire year."

The four kids stared at Chris, too stunned to respond.

"Say something," Phillips said.

"No," Dash replied. "Not until we get it all."

"Go ahead, Chris," Phillips said from the monitor above. "They've got to be prepared."

"We're not going to like this, are we?" Gabriel asked nervously.

"Retrieving each element will be difficult," Chris said. "For example, this is a creature that exists on J-16. Its image was captured by the landing probe."

On the monitor, Phillips's image gave way to a still photo of a dinosaur towering over the jungle.

Carly and Gabriel both gasped loudly.

"That's a . . . that's a . . . Raptogon!" Dash exclaimed. "The thing Anna and I battled in the arena."

"So there's intelligent life on J-16 after all," Piper said soberly.

"We have to avoid Raptogons to get the element?" Carly asked.

"Not exactly," Chris replied. "The elements that make up the Source compound are both chemical and biological. The element we need to retrieve on J-16 is the tooth of a Raptogon."

The crew erupted with stunned cries.

"You can't be serious!" Gabriel exclaimed.

"That's crazy," Carly said.

When the outburst died down, Chris said, "We have devices on board that will easily bring down a Raptogon. The challenge will be in extracting its tooth."

Dash dropped his head into his hands.

Carly's mouth fell open.

Piper held back tears.

Gabriel fought the urge to lunge at Chris and punch his lights out.

"What about the other planets?" Dash asked, his voice barely above a whisper.

"You've already gotten a taste," Phillips replied. "In the arena with the Tundra and the Meta Prime Events."

"So we weren't just being tested," Dash said. "We were being trained."

"Exactly," Phillips said.

Gabriel stood up, walked directly to Chris, and said, "So we've got to travel across the universe to get to a planet crawling with monster dinosaurs, knock one of 'em out, and then pull its tooth like Hermey the Dentist? And that's only the first element?"

"I do not understand the Hermey the Dentist reference but yes, that is the first phase of our mission."

Gabriel looked up to Phillips on the monitor and said, "Ten million bucks isn't enough."

"Is protecting Earth for generations enough?" Phillips asked.

"What else haven't you told us?" Dash asked, dead serious.

"You haven't been given the details of what must be done on each planet," Phillips said. "Other than that, yes, that is the entire extent of the mission."

"No, there is one more thing," Chris said.

"Will we hate it?" Gabriel asked.

"Quite likely," Chris replied. "With each successive planet, we will be traveling farther away from Earth. We will not be able to assemble the Source until we have retrieved all six elements. If we fail on even one of the planets, we will not be able to create the Source."

"And the mission will be a failure," Carly said.

"That is not all," Chris said. "Without the Source and the full energy it provides, the *Cloud Leopard* will not have the power to return to Earth."

That news rocked the crew, leaving them speechless as they tried to get their brains around the devastating bombshell.

"Can we turn around and go home now?" Dash asked. "Honestly."

"We cannot," Chris said. "We are at full Gamma power. It takes time to slow and we would drift past the point of no return. We must gather the elements and create the Source or we will not return to Earth."

Phillips added, "And Earth will die."

"I guess failure really isn't an option," Dash said.

The kids held a crew-only meeting in the rec room. Chris wasn't welcome, nor was STEAM.

"They've been lying to us from the beginning," Gabriel said, pacing anxiously.

"They waited until we couldn't turn back to tell us what we were in for," Carly said. "Our families have no idea."

"The whole world has no idea," Piper said.

Dash let everyone vent until there was nothing more to complain about.

"We're stuck," Dash said. "The way I see it we only have two options. We can refuse to go through with the mission. But that means we'll be lost in space. Forever."

"And the other option is to go ahead with the mission?" Piper asked.

"Yeah," Dash replied. "Maybe they're not telling the truth about getting stuck out here, but I'm not sure I want to risk that."

"I say we mutiny and take over the ship," Gabriel declared boldly. "I can plot the course and navigate us home."

"I doubt that's possible," Carly said. "Not with those ZRKs

controlling the ship. They could counter any command you programmed. Dash is right. We've only got two choices."

"Let's put it to a vote," Dash said. "We either shut it down or play it out. I vote to play it out. Remember, even with all the lies, we're here for a reason. This is about saving Earth. And our families. Gabe?"

Gabriel frowned, gave it some thought, and said, "I vote for the third choice. Mutiny. If the ZRKs stop us, then so be it, but I vote to give it a try."

"Okay. Carly?"

"We have to go ahead with the mission," she said. "It's a long shot but we still have the chance of bringing back an energy source that can stop the world from going dark. It's not what we signed up for, but hopefully the end result will be the same."

"All right, what about you, Piper?"

Piper nervously ran her hand through her long blond hair.

"I'm scared," she said. "I mean . . . dinosaurs? And who knows what's coming after that?"

"So what do you want to do?" Carly asked.

"C'mon, Piper," Gabriel said. "I can get us home."

"I believe you know how, Gabe," Piper said. "But Chris designed this ship. If we try to take control, he could probably find a way to get it back. We have to do the thing that stands the best chance of getting us home, and that's playing it out and finding the Source."

Gabriel folded his arms, pouting.

"All right, then," Dash said. "I'll tell Chris."

Dash stood at the closed door leading to Chris's quarters.

"Chris!" he called. "It's Dash."

Chris's door slid open and Dash got a glimpse into his room. The space was ringed with hard drives and monitors that rivaled the engine room of the *Cloud Leopard*. It made him realize that Piper was right: if they tried to take control of the ship, Chris would take it back.

"Yes?" Chris said.

"We all agreed to go forward with the mission, as planned," Dash said.

"I am glad to hear that," Chris said with no sign of relief or emotion. "You will not regret it."

"Yeah, we'll see. Just tell me one thing, and be honest. What do you think the odds are of us pulling this off and creating the Source?"

Chris didn't hesitate and said, "Do you want the truth?"

"Yes."

"Fifty-fifty," Chris replied. "Those odds will improve as we succeed on each planet."

The news hit Dash like a shot to the gut.

"Fifty-fifty. That's not good."

Chris didn't respond.

"I'm not going to tell the others that," Dash said. "I'm going to say you have confidence in the mission and we can't fail."

"Then you are going to be dishonest as well," Chris said. "Why is that acceptable for you, and not for me?"

"Because this wasn't my idea," Dash said, trying to hold back his anger. "I didn't ask people to leave their families and fly off on a mission that could just as easily fail as succeed. The only chance we have of pulling this off is to be confident that it's possible. So yeah, I'll fudge the truth, but that's not close to what you guys have done."

"I understand," Chris said.

Dash started to walk off, then thought of something and stopped.

"Do you know about my age? And the youth serum I'm taking?"

"I do," Chris said. "It is very brave of you."

"It's got nothing to do with being brave. I did it because I believe this mission is incredibly important and I believed in Project Alpha. Did I make a mistake?"

"Only if we fail," Chris said.

Days passed as the crew sailed through the cosmos in Gamma Speed. They continued training, now armed with information that was specific to their destination.

Gabriel flew simulations based on the footage taken by the unmanned spacecraft as it landed on J-16.

Piper studied tropical-weather illnesses and practiced with the medical kit designed to treat flesh wounds.

Carly searched the computer database to learn everything she could about J-16. Now that it was unlocked, she found a wealth of information that had been transmitted back from the unmanned craft, including data about other creatures. The Raptogon may have been the fiercest, but there were plenty of other dinosaur-like reptiles that could give them trouble.

Dash worked with the simulators as well, though he didn't fly much. Instead, he was instructed by STEAM on how to use a bazooka-like pulse cannon that fired out a charge of energy designed to topple a Raptogon. He spent hours inside a virtual-reality simulator that gave him the illusion he was in the jungle. Raptogons would appear and attack, prompting Dash to fire on them with the dummy weapon. It took him a while to get the hang of aiming the cumbersome device, but within days, he was knocking down beasties left and right.

Chris spent most of his time in his quarters and that was okay with the crew. They didn't want to deal with him. He took his meals alone and made rare appearances on the navigation deck to discuss the journey's progress.

Chris was an enigma. He had very little personality. It was like talking to an emotionless robot, which was an insult to robots that actually had a personality, like STEAM.

Rocket, on the other hand, had the run of the ship. Even though he was Chris's dog, the kids welcomed him as if he was their own. They played fetch in the gym and let him sleep across their laps while they watched movies in the rec room. Rocket turned out to be the only surprise they didn't have a problem with.

Everyone looked forward to the weekly family visits when Alpha Control patched picture and audio from their homes on Earth, directly to the ship. None of the crew let on about the truth of the mission. There was no sense in worrying their families any more than they already were. Instead, they put on happy faces and talked all about how great the ship was and demonstrated how they traveled through the tubes. Each call ended with their families feeling confident that all was well.

Like Phillips and Chris, they weren't being entirely honest.

Communication with Commander Phillips was always short, tense, and businesslike. He had lost the trust of the crew but they still needed him for ground support, making it necessary for the crew to tolerate their infrequent chats.

There was plenty to do on the ship, so it never got boring. It was when they hit the two-week mark that tension returned.

The next phase of the mission was about to begin.

Chris joined the crew on the navigation deck. When he stepped onto the bridge, everyone instantly stopped talking.

"I would like to say something," Chris announced.

Nobody responded.

"I understand your feelings toward me and toward Commander Phillips. You feel as if we deceived you and in some ways we did. But that doesn't change the reality we are faced with. Earth is in danger. Your families are in danger. We have an opportunity to save them. That's why you volunteered for this mission and that has not changed. I hope you can look beyond your disdain for our methods and remember why we are here."

"But we don't trust you," Dash said.

"I understand," Chris said. "I will do all that I can to earn that trust."

"We'll think about it," Carly said.

"Understood," Chris said. "But please think quickly."

"Why?" Gabriel asked.

Chris pointed to the endless field of stars through the forward window. For weeks, the crew had been gazing at that view, marveling at the constantly changing configuration of stars as the *Cloud Leopard* sped through the universe.

"There," Chris said. "That green light. That is J-16. We have arrived."

18

Orbit.

The rapid deceleration and exit from Gamma Speed wasn't as smooth as when they had entered. The *Cloud Leopard* bounced and buffeted as if they were flying through a turbulent sea. It pushed the crew against their safety straps, throwing them one way and then the other without warning.

"Getting sick," Piper declared.

"Is this normal?" Carly asked nervously.

Chris's image appeared on the forward monitor looking as calm as if he were relaxing in a rocking chair.

"Nothing to worry about," he said. "This won't last."

"It better not or I'm losing lunch," Gabriel said.

The thrashing lasted a few seconds longer; then the ride leveled out and it was smooth sailing once again. The crew looked to one another, waiting for somebody to say something.

"My head is still spinning," Carly said.

"So is my stomach," Piper added.

"Let's not do that again," Gabriel said while taking off his flight glasses.

"Guys," Dash said, "look."

He pointed to the forward window, where the deep green horizon of this new world stretched out before them.

"Welcome to J-16," Dash said.

There was nothing left to do except hunt down a dinosaur.

Carly gathered the crew, along with Chris and STEAM, in the recreation room. She stood in front of the monitor that showed a constantly changing collage of images of tropical jungle taken on the planet's surface.

"I've been studying J-16," she began while referring to the notes she had on her Mobile Tech Band. "I know this planet, and I know the creatures on it. I've put together a plan for going after a Raptogon. Dash and I discussed it, and he's on board."

"You talked to Dash about it and not the rest of us?" Gabriel asked.

"I'm telling you now," she replied. "I wanted to make sure my ideas made sense."

"Yeah, whatever," Gabriel said, tweaked.

An image of a Raptogon appeared on the monitor.

"We learned during the challenge at Base Ten that a Raptogon is big. It could stand as high as four stories, but it's hard to be accurate because there's no frame of reference with these images. It could be smaller."

"Or much bigger," Piper said.

"Right," Carly replied. "We also know that it's sensitive to bright light, and therefore doesn't come out during the day. It's nocturnal. That's when it hunts."

"Should we find where one of these guys sleeps and sneak up on it?" Piper asked.

"No," Carly replied. "They live deep in caves to stay out of the light. I think it would be crazy to corner one in there. We could get trapped, and they're meat-eaters."

"So that means we have to hunt it at night?" Gabriel asked. "That's almost as scary."

The image on the screen changed to a picture of a gnarly little beastie that seemed like a cross between a possum and a turtle. It had a vicious-looking pointed white face with red eyes and rows of needlelike sharp teeth. Its body was covered with a rounded shell, under which were short, stubby legs and paws with protruding claws.

"That's just disgusting," Gabriel said.

"This is the main food source for the Raptogon," Carly said. "It's about the size of a small raccoon. I call it a varmint, just because it is."

On the monitor came a video of these little creatures skittering through tall, blue-green grass. It was night and a bright light from the probe lit up the area. The varmints moved fast, with a few walking curiously up to the unmanned craft to sniff its camera with their long snouts.

"Gross," Piper said.

"They move in packs and they're fast," Carly explained. "Raptogons love munching on these little creeps."

On the monitor, a giant, scaly claw with four talons reached into the frame and snatched up a varmint. The varmint squirmed frantically, but the massive talons wrapped around it and pulled it out of frame. The next image was the monstrous clawed foot of a Raptogon. The claws were so long they couldn't be completely seen. The monster took one step directly in front of the camera, then its long, reptilian tail slid past as the Raptogon walked off with lunch.

"And that was a Raptogon," Carly said.

The others sat there, stunned.

"It's . . . really big," Piper said softly.

"This is my plan," Carly said. "Dash, Gabriel, and Piper will go down to the planet's surface. I'll stay up here and monitor the movements of the creatures and tell you their position. The first thing to do is round up as many of those little varmints as possible. We'll use them as bait. When night falls, you'll wait for the Raptogon to come looking for dinner. When the monster is close enough, Dash will hit it with the energy cannon and knock it out."

"And how do we yank the tooth?" Gabriel asked.

"I have fabricated a device," Chris said, speaking for the first time. He held up a stainless-steel contraption that had a hinge and sharp-toothed jaws. "This will clamp around one of the Raptogon's smaller front incisors. Once it's firmly fastened to the tooth, you can attach it by rope to Piper's chair. The power in that chair should be enough to extract the tooth."

"So I'm the one who has to pull it out?" Piper asked, unsure.

"Yes."

"Again, gross," Piper said with a shudder.

"What about you, genius?" Gabriel asked. "Aren't you going with us?"

"I am more valuable on the *Cloud Leopard,*" Chris replied.

"You mean because if anything happens to us, you're the uber-brain who can get to the next planet," Gabriel said.

"That is exactly right," Chris replied with no apology.

"Okay, just wanted to know where we stand," Gabriel said.

"Have you told Commander Phillips about the plan?" Piper asked.

"No," Dash replied. "As soon as we entered orbit, we lost communication."

"Seriously?" Piper asked, surprised. "We can't talk to Earth?"

Chris said, "I believe the problem is atmospheric interference from J-16."

"Who cares?" Gabriel said. "Every time we talk to that guy, he gives us bad news."

"Any questions?" Carly asked.

"Are you okay with not going down to the planet?" Piper asked. "I mean, this is what it's all about."

"I'm dying to see the dinosaurs, but I think I'm more valuable up here. So yeah, I'm okay with it."

"Five more planets to go," Dash said. "Plenty more chances to explore."

"I've got a question," Gabriel said. "How are we supposed to catch those nasty little rodents?"

Carly changed the monitor to a hand-drawn diagram that looked like a wide V on top of a rectangle.

"This is a simple drawing, but it should make sense," Carly said. "Imagine that you're looking down on it from above."

"The V is a chute," Dash said. "We'll build walls using lightweight space-blanket material." He pointed to the rectangle and added, "This is the trap we'll build out of materials from the engine room. We'll herd the varmints into the chute and force them toward the point and into the trap."

"And hope Godzilla shows up looking for dinner," Carly said.

"What if one doesn't come?" Gabriel asked.

"That shouldn't be a problem," Chris said. "The bigger worry is if more than one shows up."

The next day was spent preparing. Gabriel took the lead and used his mechanical skills to fashion a large "trap" out of lightweight mesh panels he took from the walls in the engine room. STEAM fused the seams together, and they ended up with a large square basket that was roughly the size of a small car. They created a swinging hatch on one surface that the varmints would enter through, and then it would close down to prevent them from escaping. The entire frame was hinged so it could fold together into a flat surface for transport.

Dash gathered the rest of the gear they would need. Besides his energy cannon, he brought tools to build the chute and a long length of climbing rope to pull the tooth. He found two four-foot-long rolls of silver space-blanket material that was intended to make a shelter in a survival situation, but would now be used to create the walls of the trap's chute. He also practiced with Chris's tooth clamp and made sure to bring two high-powered flashlights. With the Raptogon's sensitivity to light, he figured those lights might very well save their lives.

Piper put together a first-aid kit. She packed extra bandages and antiseptic cream for fear there would be multiple cuts from moving through the dense jungle. She also packed enough food and water to last them a day or two on the planet's surface. The *Cloud Leopard* was stocked with more than enough fruit and vegetables to last the crew for the year they would be in space. It was kept fresh in specially sealed containers.

Carly sat at a monitor in the library, scanning the planet's surface for Raptogons. She was able to detect life forms from the heat they gave off and track them as they moved. She couldn't tell what the creatures were, but she could estimate their size. The larger the heat signature, the larger the creature . . . and several large heat sources roamed the valley where the crew would land.

The equipment was loaded into the hovercraft, which was a circular, open-air, four-seat vehicle that would skim across the ground on a cushion of energy, much like Piper's wheelchair.

The hovercraft was then loaded into the bay of the *Cloud Cat*.

Within twenty-four hours of arriving in orbit, the Alpha crew was loaded and ready to go on a dinosaur hunt. The plan was to launch the *Cloud Cat* just before dawn. That would give the team a full day to build the chute and capture some varmints before the sun set and the Raptogons went on the move.

After the long day of work, the crew gathered for a final meal. The ZRKs made everyone's favorites without being asked. It was as if they knew it was a special meal.

The kids ate silently. Their minds were on the next day and the dangers they would face.

"This is wrong," Piper finally said.

"What is?" Carly asked.

"I can't live with so much tension."

She floated away from the table and zipped out of the mess hall.

The other three kids were left staring at each other in confusion.

"What was that all about?" Carly asked.

"She didn't, like, snap, did she?" Gabriel asked. "No way I'm going into dinosaur land with somebody who can't handle it. Heck, I'm not even sure *I* can handle it!"

"You can," Dash said reassuringly. "If things get dangerous, we'll just bail and figure something else out."

"Seriously?" Gabriel said. "That Raptogon hologram at Base Ten almost ate you, remember? The ones here are real. They might pass over those ugly little varmints and go right for the main course . . . us."

"And I'll knock it out," Dash said with confidence. "I'm not worried."

Carly and Gabriel exchanged looks.

They were worried.

Dash stood. "I'm going to see what's up with Piper."

He went for the door, but before he reached it, it slid open. Outside were Piper, STEAM, and Chris.

Piper floated into the room. Chris and STEAM stayed outside.

"What's going on?" Dash asked, confused.

"I don't like that we weren't told the whole truth any more than you guys do," Piper said. "But it happened and there's nothing we can do about it now."

"Yeah, so?" Gabriel said.

"So I want to get this job done and go home. If we're going to do that, we'll need help from everybody, not just the four of us. We've got a bona fide genius on board. I don't want to spend the next year being angry and pretending like he's the enemy. He needs us. That's why we're here. But we need him too. He's part of the crew, and a crew should eat together."

Dash, Carly, and Gabriel looked at one another, waiting for somebody to say something.

Carly stood up and moved her chair over, making room at the table.

"None of us have much of an appetite right now," she said to Chris. "But we always eat together because it makes us feel like we're a normal family."

Chris entered and walked slowly to the table. STEAM hung close behind him. Chris moved to the spot that Carly had cleared and looked at each of them in turn.

"Thank you," he said. "I understand how you feel about me, and I don't blame you. But I want you to know that this mission is my life. I will do everything I can to make it successful, and to get you all home safely."

"You better," Gabriel said. "Or I'm keeping your dog."

Planet J-16 was warmed by a sun similar to Earth's. As the new day arrived, bright light spread over the valley where the *Cloud Cat* would land, sending the Raptogons into their caves. When darkness returned, they would be back.

Hunting.

Gabriel sat in the pilot seat of the *Cloud Cat,* running through his preflight checklist as Carly entered.

"Hey," Gabriel said. "Why aren't you in the library scanning for monsters?"

"I wanted to wish you luck."

"Thanks. You too."

Carly looked troubled, as if she wanted to say something but wasn't sure if she should.

"What?" Gabriel asked.

"I know you don't like being told what to do," she said cautiously. "But sometimes it's good to listen."

"Okay, I'm listening."

"Not to me," Carly said. "To Dash."

Gabriel stiffened and pretended to be focused on his monitor.

"He was made commander for a reason," Carly said.

"Yeah," Gabriel shot back. "By Phillips. I'm not a big fan of his."

"I know, but Dash is smart. He always looks at stuff and tries to come up with the best answers."

"Like telling me how to fly?" Gabriel asked, annoyed.

"Well, yeah," Carly said with confidence. "And he was right."

Gabriel shot her a hurt look.

"You're an awesome pilot," Carly continued. "There's nobody I want flying us around more than you, but Dash's job is to look at the big picture. All I'm saying is don't blow him off. It might get hairy down there and I don't want to lose anybody."

Gabriel looked into Carly's eyes and saw how genuinely worried she was.

"I hear you," Gabriel said. "Teamwork and all that. Don't worry. Dash is the boss, but I'm still gonna have opinions."

Carly smiled with relief. "Wouldn't want it any other way."

"Ready to fly?" Piper said brightly as she flew up onto the flight deck.

Dash was right behind her.

"Hovercraft is secure," he announced. "Nothing left to do but get out of here."

"Good luck, guys," Carly said. "I'll be watching."

She jogged down the ramp and out of the shuttle as the others strapped into their flight seats.

"Closing up," Gabriel announced as the ramp lifted and sealed the craft.

"We're secure. Everybody set?" he asked.

Piper and Dash gave him a thumbs-up.

“Closing the air lock,” Gabriel announced.

With a whoosh of air, the heavy door that sealed off the launch bay from the rest of the *Cloud Leopard* was closed . . . and the crew went weightless.

“Opening launch doors,” Gabriel announced.

The large door at the stern of the *Cloud Leopard* slowly retracted, revealing a glorious field of stars above and the curved green horizon of J-16 below.

Gabriel put on his flight glasses and announced, “The *Cloud Cat* is on the prowl. Next stop, Jurassic Park.”

In the library, Carly, Chris, and STEAM watched a monitor with the live image from a camera mounted in the nose of the *Cloud Cat*. They were about to fly right along with them.

The shuttle lifted slowly from the deck and drifted forward.

Dash looked back to Piper and gave her an encouraging thumbs-up.

Piper returned a nervous smile.

Three hearts were beating very quickly.

The *Cloud Cat* floated through the launch doors and was soon clear of the mother ship. It drifted away for several seconds, putting distance between the two ships.

Gabriel announced, “Five seconds to insertion burn. Four . . . three . . . two . . . one. Let’s go!”

The *Cloud Cat* shot forward as its main engine kicked in. The acceleration forced the crew back into their seats as the green glow of J-16 grew larger in front of them.

“Eeehaaa!” Piper exclaimed with exhilaration.

The shuttle buffeted and jumped as it pierced the atmosphere.

Gabriel desperately wanted to take control. He glanced to Dash, who frowned and said, "Don't."

Gabriel sat back and took off his flight glasses, just to avoid the temptation.

In minutes, the force of gravity took over as the *Cloud Cat* flashed toward the ground. All eyes were on the wraparound window that gave them a panoramic view of their destination. They flew over an enormous blue ocean, which made it difficult to judge their altitude.

"Shoreline coming up," Gabriel announced.

A long strip of dark green appeared in the distance.

"There's the coast," Gabriel announced. "Five minutes until touchdown."

They flashed across the shoreline and flew over dense jungle for a minute before reaching a massive cliff, on top of which was a thick stand of tall trees.

"Once we clear the trees, we should see the valley," Gabriel announced.

The treetop canopy grew larger as they rapidly lost altitude.

"It's so beautiful," Piper said. "And totally wild."

The *Cloud Cat* was low enough that they could make out flocks of birds shooting up and out of the trees.

"I feel like we went back in time," Dash said.

"Two minutes to touchdown," Gabriel declared. "There's the valley."

Far ahead of them, the tree canopy ended and gave way to the wide, grassy valley they had all seen on the footage shot by the unmanned lander.

"Right on target," Gabriel said as the *Cloud Cat* banked automatically to the left to enter the valley and line up for landing. They were now low enough so that the two ridges of mountains that formed the valley rose above them. The navigation program was working perfectly.

Too perfectly.

"Whoa, look at that!" Gabriel exclaimed, leaning forward.

"I see it," Carly said through speakers. "That's different from the video."

Scattered across the valley floor were several tall, thick palm trees.

"They must have grown since the lander came through," Dash said.

"Yeah, well, the navigation system doesn't know that," Gabriel declared nervously. "We're going to hit those things."

He reached out to put his hand on the control pad, then glanced at Dash.

Dash reached for his flight glasses. He was about to put them on but stopped and looked at Gabriel.

Their eyes locked.

Dash pulled his hand back and commanded, "Go for it!"

Gabriel didn't have to be told twice. He threw on his glasses and slapped his hand onto the control pad.

"Taking over manual control," he declared.

They were headed straight for the largest tree.

Gabriel quickly and expertly banked the craft into a tight right turn, barely missing the tree that would have destroyed the craft.

"Yeow!" Piper exclaimed.

"I got it," Gabriel said calmly.

The *Cloud Cat* instantly gained altitude, rising above the tops of the palm trees.

"I see a window," Gabriel announced. "Hang on, I'm hitting the brakes."

The *Cloud Cat* flashed over a stand of palm trees, beyond which was a clear stretch of grass. Farther ahead were more trees.

Gabriel hit the air brakes and the deceleration was so dramatic, all three were thrown forward against their straps. Gabriel stayed focused and hit the retro-thrusters, dropping the *Cloud Cat* quickly.

"Hold tight, it might be a rough . . ."

The craft shuddered as it hit the ground.

". . . landing," Gabriel said. "Manual shutdown. System dormant and armed, ready for restart."

He looked at Dash, then at Piper, and added, "We're here."

Dash and Piper applauded. Dash leaned over for a fist bump that Gabriel returned triumphantly.

"Now *that* was some serious flying!" Dash exclaimed.

Gabriel beamed.

"That tells us something," Carly said over the radio.

"You mean that I can fly better than the computer?" Gabriel said cockily.

"Yeah, that," Carly replied. "And we can't totally rely on the info that was sent back from the unmanned probe."

Chris added, "The probe landed four years ago. There could have been many changes since then."

"Let's go out and see," Dash said.

The three unstrapped and Piper slid into her air chair. When they were set to go, they all waited in front of the hatch that would lower and become the ramp.

"We're about to step onto an alien planet," Dash said. "Except for our moon, no human beings have ever done this before."

"We should think of something historical to say," Piper offered.

"Yikes, no pressure," Gabriel said.

Dash hit the switch, and with a steady hum, the ramp lowered, settling into a grassy spot under the *Cloud Cat*.

"You're the skipper," Gabriel said. "After you."

Dash walked cautiously down the ramp and stopped at the bottom. He glanced back at the other two, who gave him nods of encouragement. Dash took a deep nervous breath and stepped onto the soft grass of planet J-16.

"This may be one small step for a man," Dash said. "But it's a heck of a long trip for a bunch of kids who are trying to save planet Earth."

Piper giggled.

Gabriel clapped. "Not bad. I wouldn't engrave it on your statue, but not bad."

Dash stepped away from the *Cloud Cat* to get his first good look at J-16.

"Wow" was all he could say.

The valley was green and lush, just as they had seen in the transmission. But unlike the images that had been beamed back and stored for years, the actual colors were so vivid it almost hurt to look at them. The blue-green grass was knee-deep and gently swayed in the warm breeze. The palm trees that had been a dangerous obstruction moments before towered high above them with cascading yellow-and-red flowers that flowed from the tops like silken rivers. The distant mountains on either side of the valley were blanketed with mossy green growth and dotted with majestic waterfalls that created a constant but distant roar. It was all crowned by a deep blue, cloudless sky that was only broken up by the occasional flock of soaring birds.

A mile behind them were the thick trees of the rain forest they had flown in over. It looked like a dark and foreboding place, compared to the bright sun-washed valley.

"It's like paradise," Piper said as she drifted up next to Dash.

"It's like Hawaii," said Dash.

"Yeah, Hawaii through a kaleidoscope," Gabriel said. "And look, we're right on the money."

He pointed off to their right, where the unmanned probe sat quietly. Vines had grown around its silver legs and wrapped themselves around the upper boxlike section that held the camera.

Dash's Mobile Tech Band flashed to life with Carly's image.

"You'd better start assembling the trap," she said. "And put on your chest cam."

It was decided that Dash would wear a camera to beam live pictures and sound back up to the *Cloud Leopard.*

"All right, let's get to work," Dash declared.

The first business was to unload the hovercraft from the *Cloud Cat.* It was a simple process with Dash controlling the vehicle while Gabriel released the clamps from inside the shuttle.

The hovercraft looked like a raft ride from an amusement park. It was round and had no roof or doors. Boarding was done by climbing over the waist-high rail. Inside were three seats and a spot for Piper's air chair.

While they worked, Piper scouted for a good spot to set the trap. She had barely gone thirty yards when she heard something skitter through the tall grass. She stopped, looked around, but saw nothing. She continued on until she saw the grass to her right shake quickly. Another rustling came from her left. Then another. And another. All around her the grass began to boil with activity.

Piper's heart raced and she turned the air chair around to head back to the *Cloud Cat* . . . when the chair was bumped from underneath. It rocked so sharply that she almost fell out. The assault continued and she had to fight to keep her balance.

"Hey!" she yelled. "Help!"

Dash and Gabriel came running, lifting their knees high to sprint through the tall grass. By the time they arrived, the attack was over.

"What's the matter?" Dash asked.

"There's something in the grass," Piper said, breathless. "It was trying to knock me out of the chair and—"

"Ow!" Gabriel screamed. "Something bit me on the ankle."

"Yeow!" Dash yelled. "Me too. What is down there?"

The grass rustled by Dash's foot. He saw a dark outline of something moving at his feet and instinctively stepped on it.

"I got it!" Dash screamed.

Without thinking, he reached down, grabbed it, and lifted it to eye level.

"It's a varmint!" Piper exclaimed.

Its snout was only inches from Dash's nose as it opened its jaws and hissed, staring him down with beady red eyes.

"Yaaa!" Dash screamed, and dropped the creature.

It hit the ground, squealed, and skittered off.

"They're all over the place!" Piper shouted.

"Back to the *Cat*!" Gabriel exclaimed, and started running.

Piper was right behind him and Dash behind her. The grass shook all around them as the creatures circled.

"The place is infested!" Gabriel yelled.

They made it to the hovercraft and dove in, headfirst. Piper swooped in and settled the air chair down onto the deck.

"Go away!" she screamed at the varmints, and hit the warning buzzer on her control pad. A loud electronic horn sounded. It was a simple device to let others know she was flying by, but it had a dramatic effect on the varmints. The creatures squealed in surprise and leapt into the air, clearing the top of the grass like popping kernels of corn.

"What the heck?" Gabriel exclaimed, trying to catch his breath.

"Again!" Dash commanded.

Piper hit the buzzer again and the creatures fled, running scared through the tall grass.

"Wow," Piper said. "Sensitive ears."

"I'm gonna enjoy serving up those little creeps to the dinosaur," Gabriel said.

"What's going on?" Carly asked through the MTB. "Any trouble?"

Gabriel said, "Nah, just getting to know the natives."

"Say again?" Carly asked, confused.

"Everything's cool," Dash said. "We're going to build the trap now."

Piper cracked open her medical kit and used antiseptic cream to clean the bites on the boys' legs before bandaging them up.

That done, the next task was to find stakes they could use to create the chute of the trap. Gabriel flew the hovercraft over the grassy plain to the stand of dense trees they had flown over on the way in.

"There's a lot of growth in there," Dash said. "That's where we'll find what we need."

When they floated into the trees and underneath the canopy, the temperature suddenly dropped ten degrees and the humidity rose dramatically.

"It's like a whole different ecosystem under here," Piper said.

Massive trees towered hundreds of feet above them, creating a dense ceiling of foliage that blocked much of the daylight. There was a constant chorus of shrieks, whistles, and coos from the birds that made their home in the tangle of branches. Thick vegetation was everywhere, either growing up from the ground or hanging down from above. Everything dripped with moisture.

"Hold up!" Dash called out.

Gabriel stopped the hovercraft. Dash grabbed a hatchet from the tool kit, leaned out over the side, and snagged a young tree. With a few quick whacks, he pulled in a five-foot-long branch.

"We'll need a dozen like this to build the chute," he said.

Gabriel guided the hovercraft in search of the raw material,

Dash leaned out and hacked them off, and Piper used a work knife to slice off smaller branches and whittle the ends into points. After only three hours, they had what they needed . . . twelve long, straight poles.

"Now what?" Gabriel asked.

"Now we build," Dash said.

Gabriel flew them out from under the jungle canopy and back toward the *Cloud Cat*.

"Let's go deeper into the valley," Dash said. "We don't want to set up anywhere near the *Cloud Cat.*"

They shot past the shuttle and sped into the valley.

"How's this?" Gabriel asked as they passed a stand of palms that guarded a wide open field.

"Perfect," Dash said.

Gabriel released the clamps that dropped the folded-up steel cage to the ground. He then landed the hovercraft and the task of assembling the trap began. Dash and Gabriel erected the cage, unfolding the car-sized trap and placing it with the hatch near the ground.

Piper set the stakes for the chute. She started at the hatch, hammering one stake into the soft ground to either side of the opening. She set the next two stakes five yards away from the cage and farther apart from each other. She repeated the process with the rest of the stakes until she created the frame of the V shape that Carly had designed. Dash and Gabriel then unrolled the lightweight silver space-blanket material and stretched it between the stakes creating two walls, one to either side of the trap. Piper used a staple gun to attach the thin material to the poles.

After a couple of hours of work in the hot sun, the trap was complete. They had created a silver funnel with five-foot-high walls that led directly to the hatch, and the trap.

"Now it's round-up time," Gabriel said.

"I haven't seen any varmints since I scared them away," Piper said.

"We need bait," Dash said. He lifted his arm and spoke into his MTB. "Carly, what do those varmints eat?"

"Stand by," Carly said. After a few minutes, she came back to say, "Roots and vegetables."

"And ankles," Gabriel said.

"All right, then," Dash said to the others. "Let's make a salad."

They spread out through the valley, gathering whatever vegetation they could find that looked appetizing. They picked rainbow-colored fruit from trees and pulled blue mushroom-looking growths up from the ground. Piper flew up high to gather juicy-looking leaves and round, pink, coconut-type fruit from the palm trees. Carly double-checked each item against her database to ensure everything they collected was edible and interesting to a varmint. Once they had enough, they placed the entire stock inside of the trap.

"Now what?" Dash asked.

"We should get out of here and let them find it," Piper suggested. "Let's come back in a couple of hours."

"What do we do in the meantime?" Gabriel asked.

Dash scanned the alien surroundings. "I don't know about you guys, but I've never been to another planet before. I'd like to take a look around."

"Yeah!" Piper said with glee.

"Now we're talking!" Gabriel exclaimed.

He flew the hovercraft deeper into the valley and closer to the base of the cliffs that towered over them. Cool mist from the waterfalls fell on their faces, taking the edge off the viciously hot tropical afternoon.

"Look at that!" Piper exclaimed.

Gabriel slowed the hovercraft in front of a giant vertical cleft in the rock face.

"It's a cave," Gabriel said.

Dash lifted his Mobile Tech Band and said, "Carly, scan the area around us. Are there any heat traces that could be a Raptogon?"

"Checking," Carly said. It only took a few seconds for her to come back and say, "Yes! There's a huge heat source coming from a spot due west of you. Get out of there!"

"It's in there," Dash said. "Go!"

Gabriel hit the throttle and the hovercraft took off.

"I can't believe I didn't bring the energy cannon," Dash said.

"No foul," Gabriel said. "Those bad boys don't come out until nightfall."

Gabriel headed all the way back to the trees that created the rain forest and flew in. Once again, they experienced the sudden change from light to darkness, from hot to cool.

"It's magical in here," Piper said.

"I never thought I'd ever see something like this," Gabriel said in awe. "Especially on the other side of the universe—"

"Look out!" Dash screamed.

Gabriel instinctively turned the hovercraft hard, barely missing a huge, moss-covered rock . . . that moved.

"Whoa!" Gabriel exclaimed, and backed the vehicle away.

The "rock" was alive. It was twenty feet high with a bear-like head and thick arms that were covered in green moss. Beneath the moss were patches of gray fur and reptilian skin. It stood up on two legs and raised its arms toward the sky.

"It's stretching," Piper said.

The creature shook like a dog drying off, then looked at the ground.

"Oh my gosh," Piper gasped.

At its feet were two identical moss creatures that were three feet tall. They wrestled with one another while playfully growling.

"It's a mother!" Piper exclaimed.

The mother reached up to an overhead branch with its massive paws and plucked a bunch of ruby-red fruit. It gently brought the food down and lovingly dropped it in front of her babies. The two hungry kids grabbed them and swallowed them whole. The mother reached up for more, but the branch was empty.

"They're hungry," Piper said.

She grabbed a plastic container holding snacks they'd brought from the ship and flew the air chair off the hovercraft.

"Whoa!" Dash yelled. "Don't!"

Dash and Gabriel watched with fear as Piper slowly floated closer to the moss family.

"Hey there," Piper called out. "I've got something for you."

The mother locked her gaze on Piper and put her arms protectively around her children.

"I'm serious, Piper," Dash called. "Don't go any closer."

Piper tossed a few apples to the creatures, then flew back into the hovercraft.

"You are nuts," Gabriel said.

"Why not make friends while we're here?" Piper said.

The mother looked down at the apples and lumbered forward, making the ground shake with her heavy footfalls.

"Get ready to blast out of here," Dash whispered to Gabriel.

"My hand's on the throttle," Gabriel replied.

The mother picked up one of the apples, raised it to her snout, and gave it a huge, sucking sniff. Satisfied, she lowered it to her kids. The bigger one got it, ate quickly, and gave off a satisfied squeak.

"I guess he likes it," Piper said, chuckling.

The mother scooped the other apples to her children, who ate them hungrily. The last apple the mother saved for herself. She popped it into her mouth, downed it, let out a satisfied growl . . . and a booming belch that shook the trees.

"Ew, gross," Piper said.

"In some cultures, that's a compliment," Gabriel said, laughing.

"I think you just made an alien friend, Piper," Dash said. "But let's not push our luck."

Gabriel throttled up and flew away from the moss beasts.

Piper waved as they moved past.

"That was awesome," she said.

"Yeah, it was," Dash admitted.

Gabriel flew deeper into the rain forest, now more wary of other beasts that might pop up and surprise them.

"There's light ahead," Gabriel announced. "We're coming to the far side of the canopy."

They emerged from the trees to see an incredible vista of yet another valley before them.

"Whoa, stop!" Dash exclaimed.

Gabriel instantly throttled down and came to a stop no more than twenty yards from the edge of the enormous cliff they had flown over on the way in.

"Yikes, that was close," Gabriel said. "This thing hovers. It doesn't fly."

The view was spectacular. They could see for miles over lush green hills that spread all the way to the distant ocean.

"There are more dinosaurs down there," Piper said.

Several gray hulks moved slowly through the vegetation far in the distance. Some had long, serpent-like necks while others were squat and fat like rhinos. A flock of red birds with ten-foot wingspans flew by so closely that the three could feel the breeze made by their beating wings.

"I wonder if this is what Earth was like," Piper said.

"It's perfect," Gabriel said. "Except no McDonald's."

They sat silently, admiring the spectacular view that no one from planet Earth had ever witnessed before and might never again.

"We better get back and check the trap," Dash finally said.

They retraced their trip back through the rain forest. When they broke out into the sunlight on the far side, Gabriel throttled up and brought them straight to the trap.

"Nothing," Dash said as he gazed through the wire mesh at the untouched pile of fruit and vegetables.

"I guess they're not as dumb as they look," Gabriel said.

Piper looked up at the sky to see the sun inching closer to the distant mountaintops.

"We don't have a lot of time," she said.

Dash looked out across the valley.

"They're out there," he said. "I see the grass moving."

"So how do we get them in here?" Gabriel asked.

"I have an idea," Piper declared.

Five minutes later, Dash and Gabriel sat in the hovercraft fifty yards to the right of the mouth of the chute. Piper sat on her air chair fifty yards in the other direction. Dash waved to her. Piper waved back.

Dash pushed a button that triggered a high-pitched warning siren. Piper did the same on her air chair. Both vehicles moved slowly toward one another.

The stretch of grass between them boiled with the frantic movement of hundreds of varmints. The sound was driving them crazy . . . and driving them away.

"Get along, little doggies!" Gabriel called out. "Eeeehaaa!"

"It's working!" Piper yelled.

Gabriel and Piper carefully maneuvered their vehicles closer, pushing the varmints together and forcing them toward the mouth of the chute. Gabriel made quick movements back and forth, trying to appear as large as possible to keep them from running past. Piper did the same. Many varmints skittered away but just as many bashed their way into the silver chute as they fled from the torturous sound.

The hovercraft and the air chair drew close to one another. The grass inside the chute boiled with frantic varmints. There was nowhere for them to go but through the hatch and into the cage. Soon, the metal sides of the trap began to rattle.

"We got 'em!" Piper declared.

Dash jumped over the side of the hovercraft and ran for the trap. Varmints dashed around his feet but he ignored them. He made it to the point of the chute, slammed that hatch shut, and threw his arms up in triumph.

Gabriel and Piper turned off their sirens. The loud horns gave way to the sounds of thirty angry varmints thrashing around inside the cage.

"And the trap is set," Piper declared.

Gabriel pointed to the distant range of mountains. "Not a minute too soon."

The sun dipped below the ridge, casting the valley into shadow.

The Raptogons would soon be on the prowl.

20

The crew returned to the *Cloud Cat* to eat some food and prepare for the main event. The tooth clamp was secured inside the hovercraft next to the long coil of climbing rope. The two high-powered flashlights were placed on the deck, ready to be grabbed when needed. Most importantly, Dash prepared the energy cannon. It was a long silver device with a double bore and a metal half ring in back that fit around his shoulder. "You sure you know how to handle that thing, pardner?" Gabriel asked.

"No problem," Dash assured him. "It's got a kick, but I guess you need a serious kick to knock down something that big."

"Do me a favor?" Gabriel asked.

"What's that?

"Don't miss."

Darkness arrived quickly. The only light in the valley came from the glow of the billions of stars in the night sky. The three boarded the hovercraft and floated into the valley, where Gabriel landed the vehicle fifty yards from the mouth of the trap. Once in position, they powered down, settled in, and waited. And waited.

And waited some more.

Every so often, Gabriel would hit the warning horn on the hovercraft. The shrill sound woke the trapped varmints, who would chatter and squeal for ten minutes before settling down again. The idea was to let any nearby Raptogon know that dinner was served.

"You think one of those stars is home?" Piper asked, looking skyward.

"Probably," Dash said.

"It's that one," Gabriel said. "Or maybe that one. No, wait, I'll bet it's that one. Or maybe any one of the billions out there."

"Kinda makes you feel small, doesn't it," Piper said wistfully.

"Not small," Dash said. "More like . . . proud. One of those stars out there is ours and we're trying to save it. Not a lot of people can say that."

"Four to be exact," Gabriel said. "Five if you count that Chris dude."

"He counts," Piper said. "If not for him, we wouldn't be here."

"Not sure if that's a good or a bad thing," Gabriel said with a scoff.

"It's a good thing," Dash said with certainty. "You know you want to be here. We all do."

"Yeah, but I didn't expect to be out in the dark hunting dinosaurs," Gabriel said.

"Be honest," Dash said. "If you knew before, about the dinosaurs and all the stops we had to make and the danger, would you still have volunteered?"

Gabriel was about to give a quick answer, but stopped to give it some serious thought.

Piper said, "Maybe I'm weird, but I think that makes it even better. That mossy mother monster today was incredible."

Gabriel finally said, "Okay, fine. Yeah, I'd still be here. But ask me again in the morning. I might have a different opinion."

"Wake up, guys," Carly's voice said through the Mobile Tech Bands. She sounded agitated.

"We're here," Dash replied. "What's up?"

"I'm picking up a large heat signature," she answered. "It's deeper in the valley and on the move."

All three kids were suddenly wide awake.

"Any others?" Dash asked.

"No. That's the only one within twenty miles. I can't guarantee it's a Raptogon but whatever it is, it's big. I mean really big. And it's headed your way."

"And here we go," Gabriel said.

Dash grabbed the energy cannon, fixed it over his shoulder, and rested his elbows on the outer rail of the hovercraft.

"Grab the lights," Dash instructed. "When I tell you, turn them on and hit the Raptogon in the eyes. That'll confuse him and give me a target."

"Are we close enough to the trap?" Piper asked.

"I don't know," Dash replied. "Better safe than stupid. I don't want to get squished."

"You don't want to miss either," Gabriel said gravely.

They waited, quietly, tuned for any telltale sign that trouble was on the way.

There was nothing.

"Maybe it's a storm cloud," Piper suggested. "It could be floating this way and—"

The hovercraft shook.

It was slight, but it shook.

"Did you feel that?" Gabriel asked.

"No," Piper replied. "What was it?"

Seconds later, the hovercraft shook again.

"I felt that," Dash declared nervously.

The craft trembled. It was short and quick, but it was real.

Dash said, "It's either mini earthquakes—"

"Or footsteps," Gabriel declared. It was tough to hide the tension in his voice.

Dash settled in behind the energy cannon and looked down the twin barrels.

"Can't see a thing," he said. "Get ready with the lights."

The ground shuddered several more times.

"Whatever it is," Piper said, "it's coming closer."

The varmints started squealing.

"I hear it," Gabriel announced, squinting in concentration. "It's moving through the grass."

They heard a loud crack, followed by a sharp thump.

"And the trees," Dash said. "It's crushing anything in its path."

The quakes came quicker and sounded more violent.

"It must hear the varmints," Piper said. "It wants to eat."

"Come and get it, Rapper," Gabriel cajoled. "We got dinner for you, and a very big surprise."

Several more tremors followed.

"My heart is thumping," Piper said with a thin, nervous voice.

"I think I see it," Dash declared. "Or I can see where it's blocking out the stars. Man, it's big."

"Tense up, buddy," Gabriel said. "Don't miss. You promised."

Two more thundering quakes shook the craft, followed by nothing. Everything went still. The only sound came from the squealing varmints.

The three held their breaths, waiting, until a new sound emerged.

"What is that?" Piper whispered. "It sounds like . . . wind."

They listened closely, trying to recognize what it might be.

"Oh man," Gabriel finally said, barely above a whisper. "We're hearing it breathe."

The quiet night was suddenly shattered by the sound of wrenching metal and the squeals of frantic varmints.

"It got the trap!" Piper declared. "It's right there!"

"Light it up!" Dash yelled.

Piper and Gabriel switched on the high-powered lights and shot them toward the violent sounds. When the beams hit the target . . .

Piper screamed.

Gabriel did too.

"Oh man!" Dash exclaimed, stunned.

The Raptogon was right in front of them. It was three times the size of the hologram at Base Ten, standing a hundred and fifty feet high. Its clawed foot was as large as the hovercraft. The beast towered over the silver chute with the metal cage dangling from its giant front claws.

Dash couldn't breathe. The sight of the massive creature brought back frightening memories . . . times three. Sweat rolled down his forehead and dripped into his eyes.

"Hit its face!" he commanded, breathless.

Piper and Gabriel had to hold the big flashlights with two hands to keep them steady as they directed the beams at the monster's eyes. The beast let out a blood-chilling scream as if it had been hit by lasers. It immediately let go of the trap and held its clawed hands up to shield its eyes. The cage plummeted to the ground, broke apart, and freed the varmints.

"Shoot it!" Gabriel screamed.

Dash was frozen. The sight of the behemoth went beyond any nightmare he could imagine. He desperately wiped sweat from his eyes and tried to line up a shot.

"C'mon, Dash," Piper said with incredible calm. "You can do it."

Dash's hands trembled. He feared he wouldn't be able to hold the cannon steady enough to get off a good shot.

The beast howled and focused its attention on the source of its agony. The hovercraft. It leaned down low, loomed dangerously close to the crew, and let out a horrifying scream that rumbled their bellies.

Dash could feel its hot breath on his face. It petrified him so completely that he couldn't move.

"You gotta shoot, Dash," Piper said coolly.

The beast stood up again and opened its long snout to reveal multiple rows of sharp teeth. It howled as if gathering strength from the pain, focused on the hovercraft . . .

. . . and charged.

When its foot hit the ground, the impact thundered the world so violently that the vehicle bounced.

"Dash!" Gabriel screamed. "Drop this sucker!"

Seeing the beast headed their way rocked Dash back into the moment and cleared his head. He looked down the long barrel of the silver cannon, zeroing in on the monstrous head.

He would get only one shot.

"Do it!" Piper screamed.

"Good night," he said, and pulled the trigger.

The powerful device chugged in Dash's grip, pushing him back into the hovercraft.

The bolt of energy sprang from the barrel, flashed through the night sky and found its mark. The monster stopped in its tracks. Its whole body twisted, as if trying to move away from this strange, invisible attack that came out of the dark. Too late. The Raptogon was still on its feet, but it was unconscious. It teetered and fell.

"Timber!" Gabriel yelled.

The monster hit the ground with such a thunderous jolt that the hovercraft bounced and nearly flipped over. The head of the beast came to rest not twenty yards from them.

"Gee," Gabriel said to Dash. "You think you could have cut that a little closer?"

"Sorry," Dash said. "I didn't expect it to be so . . . so . . ."

"Scary?" Piper asked.

"That's a good word," Dash replied, wiping the sweat from his forehead.

The three stared at the downed monster, their light beams playing across its head.

“We’re lucky it didn’t land on us,” Piper said.

Dash dropped the cannon and went for the metal clamp and the rope.

“Let’s do this before it wakes up,” he said.

He leapt over the side, followed right behind by Gabriel, who continued to train the flashlight beam on the monster. The blinding light that cowed the beast had now become a work light.

Dash ran to its head, but stopped a few feet away to stare in awe at the frightening, majestic animal.

It lay on its side, its head rising up several feet higher than Dash and Gabriel. The skin of the monster was a mass of slimy gray-green scales. Its breathing was steady but labored. It was a reminder that the beast wasn’t dead, only unconscious.

“It’s amazing,” Dash said in wonder.

“Yeah, and if it wakes up, we’re breakfast,” Gabriel said. “Can we do this please?”

Dash knelt down next to the mouth and reached out to grasp a handful of lip skin.

“This is disgusting,” he said.

As he lifted the heavy lip away from the gum, there was a wet, smacking sound. Sticky saliva was everywhere, creating a suction that made it difficult to keep the lip separated.

“Give me a hand,” Dash said.

“Do I have to?” Gabriel asked as he grabbed the lip and lifted it high, revealing a long row of large, lethal teeth.

“Take your pick,” Gabriel said. “Just do it fast.”

Dash went to work with the clamp. He found one upper tooth that had enough space on either side to insert the clamp.

He loosened the metal frame, wrapped it around the sharp tooth, then tightened the device down. With a couple of sharp tugs, he was satisfied that it wouldn't come loose.

"This is nuts," Gabriel said. "Dino dental work on the far side of the universe. That'll be the name of the book I write."

Dash quickly reached for the climbing rope, threaded it through the eye in the clamp, and tied it off. Again, a couple of quick tugs told him it was secure.

"Ready for me?" Piper asked as she backed her air chair toward them.

Dash played out twenty yards of line and tied off the other end to a hook on the back of the air chair. He looped the remaining coil around the same hook.

"That's it," he declared. "Back up about halfway, then throttle up to get some power. By the time the rope goes taut, there should be enough force to yank the tooth."

"You think it will hurt him?" Piper asked.

"Who cares?" Gabriel exclaimed.

"He's only got a couple of hundred others," Dash said. "He won't miss one."

Dash guided the air chair backward, letting the rope go slack.

"That's good," he said. "Ready?"

Piper nodded.

Dash backed away to stand with Gabriel, who kept the beam of light on the monster's mouth.

"All right," Dash called out. "Anytime."

Piper took a deep breath. She grasped the side of her air

chair with one hand for balance and put her other hand on the joystick.

"Here we go," she declared. "Three . . . two . . . one . . ."

She hit the throttle and the air chair leapt forward.

The rope went taut.

The air chair groaned.

The tooth didn't budge.

The beast's eyes snapped open.

Piper gunned the throttle but she was stuck, attached to a tooth that wasn't going anywhere and to a beast who didn't like it one bit.

"It's awake!" Gabriel shouted. "Cut the rope!"

Dash ran for the air chair, fumbling to get the work knife out of his belt.

Too late.

The beast's head snapped up and yanked the air chair along with it. The sudden force flipped Piper out, sending her tumbling to the grass below.

"Piper!" Dash yelled.

"What's going on?" Carly called through Gabriel's Mobile Tech Band. "What's happening?"

Nobody answered. They were frozen in fear, staring up at the monster as it rose to its feet. The rope with the useless air chair dangled below its mouth.

It was hurt. It was angry.

It wanted revenge.

21

"What's happening?" Carly cried.

She sat at her monitor in the library, frantic. On-screen was a jumble of confusing images sent back from Dash's chest cam. An arm, a blur of grass, a flash of light from the high-intensity beams, Piper's frightened face, the hovercraft, and then a giant reptilian foot smashing down.

Chris watched over her shoulder, along with STEAM. Rocket sat at their feet, whimpering nervously.

"The air chair did not have the power to extract the tooth," Chris said with surprising calm. "That was my miscalculation. I should have recommended using the hovercraft."

"They're on the run!" Carly shouted on the edge of panic. "We have to do something."

"Agreed," Chris said, and hurried toward the tube.

Rocket barked and tried to run after him.

"Where are you going?" Carly yelled.

Chris quickly entered a destination and jumped in.

"Chris!"

"Fire up the hovercraft!" Dash shouted.

Gabriel backed quickly toward the craft while shining the light beam at the Raptogon.

The Raptogon was too enraged to care. The light was nothing more than an annoying mosquito buzzing around its head. It grabbed at the air chair that dangled from his tooth and pulled on it. All it managed to do was release the remaining length of rope so that the air chair now hung close to the ground, bouncing around its feet.

Dash ran for Piper and fell to his knees beside her.

"Are you hurt?" he asked.

"I don't think so," she replied, dazed.

Dash scooped her up and looked back to see the Raptogon was headed their way.

"Don't trip," Piper said with amazing cool.

Dash took off running, headed for the hovercraft.

The Raptogon stormed after them.

Gabriel was already on board and powered up.

"Move!" he screamed.

Dash made it to the craft and handed Piper up to Gabriel. Gabriel planted her in a seat and handed her the flashlight.

"Better than nothing," he said.

Piper shone it back at the oncoming monster.

It didn't slow the charge at all.

"Go!" Dash screamed as he climbed aboard.

Gabriel didn't wait for him to be all the way in. He lifted the vehicle up off the grass, spun one hundred and eighty degrees, and hit the throttle. The round machine took off and flew quickly over the valley floor as Dash fell onto the deck.

"I need light!" Gabriel shouted. "I can't see where we're going."

Piper spun around and directed the beam ahead . . . in time to light up a palm tree directly in their path.

"Yeow!" Gabriel screamed as he banked hard to the left, barely avoiding disaster.

Dash went for the energy cannon. He picked up the long silver device and fixed it on his shoulder.

"Take him down!" Gabriel shouted.

Dash fired and missed.

"Again!" Piper demanded.

Dash fired at the same instant Gabriel had to skirt another palm tree. It threw his aim off and another shot went wild.

The Raptogon kept coming.

"Shoot!" Piper yelled.

"I can't," Dash cried. "It takes time to recharge."

"We're going back to the shuttle," Gabriel announced. "We'll launch back to the *Cloud Leopard* and figure something else out."

"Can you take off before that thing reaches us?" Dash asked.

"I think so. If I do a hot start from the hard drive, I can—"

Gabriel's words caught in his throat when he saw that the *Cloud Cat* was powering up on its own. Lights shone below and the engines whined.

"Tell me you're doing that," Piper said.

"I . . . I . . . no," Gabriel said, stammering.

The engine whine grew louder and the *Cloud Cat* lifted straight up off the valley floor.

Dash went right to his MTB and screamed, "Carly, what's going on? The *Cloud Cat* just took off by itself!"

Carly replied, "I . . . I don't know. Chris left me here alone. It must be him."

"Chris," Gabriel said, spitting out the word. "He's saving his toy spaceship and hanging us out to dry."

Dash looked back to see that the Raptogon was closing the distance between them.

The monster howled angrily, desperate for revenge.

"We can't stay out in the open," Dash said. "He'll chase us down. Head back for the rain forest. Maybe we can lose it in there."

"Seriously?" Gabriel said. "I can barely see anything out here. It'll be zero visibility under those trees."

"I'm open to better ideas," Dash said.

Gabriel thought, then changed direction for the rain forest, pushing the hovercraft to the limit of its speed. Piper kept the powerful light beam focused ahead. It kept them from hitting any trees . . .

. . . and let the Raptogon know exactly where they were.

The boundary of trees that marked the beginning of the rain forest could barely be seen in the distance. Gabriel hit the throttle and blasted for it.

"Maybe when we get in there, it'll give up," Piper said hopefully.

"Maybe," Dash said, though he didn't believe it.

Gabriel throttled back and slipped past the first line of trees that marked the beginning of the dense jungle.

"I gotta slow down," he said. "Or we'll crash for sure."

He flew the hovercraft as quickly as he felt was safe.

It wasn't quick enough.

The Raptogon didn't worry about dodging trees. It crushed

them. The monster charged into the thick jungle, crunching vegetation under its huge, clawed feet.

"It's not giving up," Gabriel said.

"Let's find a place to hide," Dash commanded.

Gabriel maneuvered around a thick stand of gnarly trees, hoping it would put them out of sight. He hit the accelerator and sped ahead.

"There!" Piper called out.

Ahead was a mound of trees and vines that formed a large cave that was twice the size of the hovercraft. Gabriel sped toward it, staying low to the jungle floor.

"Kill the light," he commanded.

Piper turned off the beam and Gabriel flew the last hundred yards from memory into the cave. They floated inside, turned back around to face out, and settled to the ground.

Dash quickly positioned himself in front of the hovercraft with the energy cannon while Gabriel shut down every light on board.

"Is the cannon recharged?" Piper whispered.

"I think so," Dash whispered back.

The pounding footfalls could no longer be heard.

"It stopped," Piper whispered.

"We must have lost it," Gabriel said.

"But it's still out there," Dash cautioned.

The Raptogon was still moving, but more cautiously as it searched for its prey. The distant sound of less frantic footfalls were heard as it shuffled through the dense foliage.

A minute went by. Two minutes.

Then there was nothing.

No sound. No movement.

"Is it gone?" Piper asked.

"I just thought of something," Gabriel whispered. "If its eyes are so sensitive to light, does that mean it can see in the dark?"

As if to answer, the Raptogon bellowed and charged for them. It was only fifty yards away.

"I guess it can see in the dark," Dash exclaimed.

Piper screamed as its giant foot stomped down, thirty yards away.

Dash fumbled to aim the energy cannon as . . .

"Look out!" Gabriel screamed.

From behind them, a dark shape charged out from the depths of the cave. The shadow stampeded past and galloped directly for the Raptogon, bellowing and chuffing like an enraged rhino.

"What the heck is that?" Dash yelled.

"It's the mother!" Piper exclaimed.

The moss creature hurled itself at the Raptogon's leg, wrapped its thick arms around the ankle, and bit at its scaly flesh.

"Get us out of here!" Dash yelled to Gabriel.

Gabriel fired up the engines and sped out of the cave.

Piper flashed the beam of light onto the battle in time to see the Raptogon shaking its leg to try to get rid of the moss creature.

"She saved us," Piper said.

The Raptogon gave a mighty flick of its leg and the moss mother went flying off into the dark jungle.

"I hope she's okay," Piper said.

"Seriously?" Gabriel shouted. "That's what you're worried about?"

Piper redirected the light ahead of them, lighting up the labyrinth of trees they had to fly through.

"It's not gonna give up," Dash said. "We can't outrun it forever."

"We can't outrun it at all," Gabriel announced. "Our batteries are nearly dead."

"No!" Piper moaned.

The hovercraft bucked as its engine slowed. Gabriel pushed it until they cleared the trees on the far side of the rain forest. There was a thirty-yard stretch of grass from the edge of the trees to the cliff, and a half-mile fall to the jungle far below.

"It's okay," Dash declared. "We're better off on foot. The hovercraft was too easy to follow."

"You know my chair is gone, right?" Piper said.

"I'll carry you," Dash replied. "Hop on my back and—"

The Raptogon crashed out of the trees and onto the bluff, directly over them.

Dash looked around, desperate to find the energy cannon.

The Raptogon shook its head, making the air chair on the end of the long rope swing wildly.

Dash spotted the cannon and dove for it . . .

. . . as the air chair hit him in the back, knocking him over the rail and out of the hovercraft.

Gabriel leapt right out after him.

"I got you, man," he said as he helped a stunned Dash to his feet.

Piper crawled for the cannon and lifted it toward the Raptogon. She swung it around, aimed, and pulled the trigger but the device wasn't anchored and it knocked her back down onto the deck of the hovercraft.

The shot didn't even come close to hitting the Raptogon.

Warm drool dripped on them from high above. The Raptogon was hungry—and angry. It lifted its heavy foot, ready to stomp the life out of its tormentors.

There was nothing they could do but cower.

"Man, I can't believe it's going to end like this," Gabriel said.

Suddenly, a bright light shone down on them from the sky. The brilliant beam hit the face of the Raptogon, making it thrash its head back and forth to protect its eyes.

Their Mobile Tech Bands flashed to life.

"Get to the trees," a voice said calmly.

The kids all looked at their wrists with dismay.

It was Chris.

Piper looked to the sky, shielding her eyes against the bright beam.

"It's the *Cloud Cat*!" she exclaimed.

The beam of light blasted from the nose of the shuttle as it circled above the head of the monster.

"You have ten seconds to protect yourselves," Chris said. "I'm going to fire on the Raptogon."

"The *Cat* has weapons?" Gabriel asked in surprise.

"How did you get on board?" Dash yelled into his MTB.

"I am not on board," Chris said. "I am controlling it from the *Cloud Leopard*."

The Raptogon swung its head, fighting the pain-inducing beam of light.

Dash saw the air chair swinging near them. This time he was ready for it.

"Get Piper into the trees," he commanded.

Gabriel scrambled to his feet and leaned into the hovercraft.

"Let's go!" he yelled to Piper.

Piper crawled to him, dragging her legs. Gabriel grabbed her under the arms and pulled her out.

"Where's Dash?" she asked.

"He's coming."

He wasn't coming.

Dash crouched down next to the hovercraft for protection. His eyes were on the swinging air chair.

Suddenly, the moss creature once again leapt out from the trees.

The mother wasn't giving up either. She grabbed the Raptogon's leg and gnashed at its ankle. The Raptogon wailed and fell to one knee.

Dash dove out of the way and barely missed being crushed by the dinosaur's knee as it crashed to the ground. He didn't stop to think about how close he had come to being jelly. He looked around frantically until he saw what he hoped for: the air chair was on the ground. The rope was slack because the Raptogon was down on its knee.

"You need to move, Dash," Chris said calmly.

"Give me ten more seconds," Dash replied.

He scrambled to his feet and ran for the air chair. He was frighteningly close enough to the Raptogon to touch its scaly skin but he stayed focused. He got to the air chair, flipped it over, and hopped on.

“Please don’t be busted,” he said under his breath.

He pulled up on the joystick and the chair lifted off.

“Yes!”

He looked around quickly and saw a thick tree with a double-trunk that rose up in a V shape. Perfect. He flew the chair toward it, passed through the V shape, and circled through once again . . . wrapping the rope around one side of the tree.

“Get out of there, Dash,” Chris warned.

Dash jumped off the chair, letting it fall into the crook of the tree.

The moss creature was still clamped onto the Raptogon’s leg. The huge monster reached down and swatted it away, sending it careening back into the forest. The behemoth then rose back onto its feet and tried to stand straight, but the rope went taut, preventing it from standing to its full height.

Dash sprinted into the woods, jumped over a fallen log, and hid behind it.

“Let him have it!” he shouted into his MTB.

The *Cloud Cat*’s front cannons erupted, sending powerful blasts of energy toward the Raptogon. Each cannon was ten times more powerful than the device Dash had used to bring down the beast. But Chris wasn’t targeting the Raptogon. He was shooting at the ground between the giant and the trees.

Dash got up, ran to the others, and jumped down next to them.

“Nobody told me the *Cat* had claws,” Gabriel said.

“He’s not aiming at the Raptogon,” Piper said. “What is he doing?”

The pulverizing onslaught continued. Round after round of energy went into the ground, blasting geysers of dirt into the air that rained down on the others.

The Raptogon desperately tried to back away but the rope attached to the tree kept him from moving. It fought against the line but that only wedged the air chair tighter into the crook of the tree. The high beam of light continued to keep it off balance as the barrage of energy blasted away at its feet.

"Why doesn't he just shoot it?" Gabriel asked.

The answer came a few seconds later.

The ground shook, but not from the Raptogon.

There was a low, wrenching rumble as the ground beneath the monster gave way. The cliff was collapsing. The Raptogon reached out to grab onto something. Too late. Most of the shelf that was the overlook gave way and the Raptogon fell. It clawed desperately at the disintegrating cliff but the loose dirt crumbled under its grasp.

With a gut-wrenching scream, the Raptogon fell.

The three kids sat huddled together, not moving until they heard the distant crash as the Raptogon landed in the jungle below. They sat that way for a solid minute, wanting to make sure that the beast was truly gone.

"Is it over?" Piper asked.

They saw movement off to their right and cowered in fear.

Standing over them with its front paws on the rocks they were hiding behind was the moss creature. It was out of breath and barely able to stand.

"There's definitely intelligent life on J-16," Dash said.

Piper raised her hand and waved as if to say "thank you."

The mother got the message, turned away, and shuffled back into the jungle to find her children.

"Didn't see that coming," Gabriel said. "Didn't see any of this coming."

Dash crawled toward the cliff and stopped at the line of trees.

"You gotta see," he called to the others.

Three-quarters of the land that had been the overlook was gone. The edge of the cliff had moved twenty yards closer. The hovercraft sat teetering on the edge.

From the valley far below, they heard the cry of the Raptogon. It was alive, but it was no longer a threat.

The *Cloud Cat* floated overhead, shining its beam of light down on the kids.

"Is everyone all right?" Chris asked through the MTB.

"We're okay," Dash said.

"I will find a safe place to land," Chris said. "In the meantime, pull up the rope."

The *Cloud Cat* flew off, hugging the cliff.

"Rope?" Gabriel asked. "What's he talking about?"

Dash realized immediately.

"Help me," he said as he crawled over some rocks to get to the tree that had the air chair wrapped around it.

Gabriel joined him and saw that the rope was still attached to the air chair, and dangled over the cliff.

"Is it possible?" Gabriel asked.

They both grabbed the rope and worked together to pull it up.

"It's heavy," Gabriel said.

They pulled for what felt like an eternity, their arms burning from the strain. Just before they had reached the limit of their endurance, they hoisted up the heavy object that was attached to the other end.

Piper crawled up to them and saw the gleaming metal frame that was wrapped around the heavy load.

"Guess he'll be chewing on the other side of his mouth for a while," Piper said.

Gabriel laughed.

Piper did too.

Dash laughed the hardest.

They had done it.

The three fell down on top of one another, giddy with relief and the knowledge that they had completed one-sixth of their mission.

The tooth was theirs.

22

The air-lock doors opened to reveal Dash, Piper, and Gabriel standing in the launch bay in front of the *Cloud Cat.* All three were covered in dirt and their clothes were torn and filthy. Dash was giving Piper a piggyback. They looked as though they had been through a war.

Because they had.

Waiting for them in the engine room were Carly, STEAM, and Chris.

"J-16," Gabriel announced. "Nice place to visit. Wouldn't want to live there."

Carly ran up and pulled them into a group hug.

"I thought you were all done," she said.

"We were," Dash said. "About ten times over. We finally ran out of luck until Chris showed up."

"You all performed in an exemplary manner," Chris said with surprisingly little emotion. "From setting that trap and bringing down the Raptogon to Dash's quick thinking in pulling the tooth. Congratulations."

"Thanks," Dash said to Chris.

"You can control the *Cloud Cat* from up here?" Gabriel asked.

"I can," Chris replied.

STEAM walked up, pushing along another air chair.

"Good thing we have spares, yes sir," the robot said.

Dash gently lowered Piper onto the floating chair.

Several ZRKs flew by them and headed into the launch bay to give the *Cloud Cat* a once-over.

Chris said, "When daylight returns, I will fly down to the planet's surface to retrieve the tooth and the hovercraft."

"Need any help?" Gabriel asked.

"No."

"Good, because I'm not going down there again."

"Again, congratulations to you all," Chris said. "I will allow you to celebrate."

He turned to walk off.

"Wait!" Piper called. "You're part of this crew too."

Chris wasn't sure of how to respond.

"C'mon, man," Dash said. "If not for you, we'd still be down there and it wouldn't be pretty."

"You wish for me to join in your celebration?" Chris asked, surprised.

"Geez, don't make it sound so exciting," Gabriel said.

"Of course we do," Piper replied.

"Very well," Chris said with the slightest of smiles. "Meet me in the dining area in an hour. I will prepare a surprise."

Chris headed off for the tube.

"I'm not so sure I want any more of his surprises," Gabriel said uneasily.

Carly took a step back from the group and gave them a quick once-over.

"You guys are a mess," she said, half laughing.

"Yeah," Gabriel said. "But we are *bad.*"

"Yeah we are!" Piper exclaimed with joy.

Gabriel added, "And we've got a steely-eyed commander who pulled this thing out, along with a very big tooth. Awesome, man. Just awesome."

He held up his fist and Dash gratefully bumped knuckles.

"It was a team effort," Dash said modestly.

An hour later, the crew entered the dining area and were surprised to see that the table was covered with a colorful spread of cookies, cakes, and pies.

"Wow!" Piper exclaimed. "He wasn't kidding!"

Chris entered in a rush from the galley with his uniform covered in flour.

"This was all I could manage in an hour," he said.

"How is this possible?" Gabriel asked, stunned.

Chris said, "I work fast . . . and most of it was ready-made."

"So you're a genius *and* a great cook?" Carly exclaimed.

Chris shrugged. "I am."

Gabriel jumped into a seat, scanning the array of sweets. "If you cook stuff like this the rest of the trip, I just might forgive you for everything. That's a big *if,* so don't coast."

Everyone took spots at the table and dug in, grabbing towering slices of chocolate cake and steaming-hot slices of blueberry pie. Even Rocket got a slice of cake. Chris joined them and ate a single piece of pie as he listened to the group relive the adventure on J-16.

"So what happens now?" Dash asked Chris.

"I will bring back a section of the tooth that Carly will put into the Element Fuser to break down into Rapident Powder . . . the first element of the Source."

"Rapident Powder?" Dash asked. "How did you figure this all out?"

Chris paused before answering, as if he'd hoped the question hadn't been asked.

"It came after years of experimentation."

"Yeah, but pulverized Raptogon tooth?" Gabriel said skeptically. "How random is that?"

"And it is only the first of six elements," Chris said, ignoring the line of questioning.

The crew fell silent. Reality had returned.

"Where do we go next?" Carly asked.

Chris wiped his mouth with a napkin and stood up.

"Enjoy today," he said. "There will be plenty of time to worry about tomorrow. Good night, and once again, congratulations on a job well done."

He left with Rocket padding after him as the others wished him a good night.

Early the next morning, while the crew slept, Chris entered the *Cloud Cat* along with several ZRKs. He expertly guided the craft out of the launch bay and flew straight for the surface of J-16. He landed the craft on the newly cut cliff. The sun was up and spreading its golden warmth over the landscape. When the hatch opened, the ZRKs quickly went to work. They ran power lines from the *Cloud Cat* to the hovercraft to charge its batteries.

Others swarmed the damaged air chair. They pried it loose and flew it into the *Cloud Cat.*

As the ZRKs worked, Chris went right to the massive Raptogon tooth that lay in the grass. It was the size of a washing machine, with an added point on the business end. Chris pulled off the metal clamp and went to work with a small power saw. He first removed the bulk of the root from the sharp end of the tooth. He then sawed the root in half. The root is what was needed to create the Rapident Powder. Knowing he had more than enough in a piece that was the size of a classroom desk, he left the remaining half of the root on the bluff.

Once the root was stowed safely aboard the *Cloud Cat,* Chris left the shuttle again and hopped aboard the hovercraft. After the ZRKs disengaged the charging cables, Chris floated it into the rain forest.

He sped over fallen logs and twisted vines, slowing as he passed the cavern where Dash, Piper, and Gabriel hid from the charging Raptogon. He settled the hovercraft down inside a massive footprint that was left by the beast the night before. He looked at the deep indentation and shuddered. If that monster had hurt the kids, he never would have forgiven himself.

He had to force that image out of his head for he was on a mission. He walked boldly into another nearby cavern as if he knew exactly where he was going. He used the flashlight on his Mobile Tech Band to show him the way. He kicked past several rocks and what looked like bones from some dinosaur's previous meal until he came to three bowling-ball-sized rocks arranged in a triangle. They looked as though they hadn't been touched in decades, which gave him a sigh of relief.

He pushed the rocks away and dug with his hands in the soft dirt. Six inches below the surface, he struck metal. He dug even faster and moments later pulled out a metal container the size of a shoe box. He brushed off the dirt, clutched the box under his arm, and started back for the hovercraft. He retraced his route to the cliff, loaded the hovercraft to the *Cloud Cat,* and lifted off.

He was back on board the *Cloud Leopard* before the rest of the crew had even woken up . . . with a precious souvenir from J-16 that nobody knew existed . . . except for Chris.

"It's kind of gross," Piper said.

They watched with fascination as Carly maneuvered the tooth root inside the oven-like receptacle of the Element Fuser.

Nobody was watching with more intensity than Chris. He wanted no mistakes.

Carly followed her checklist, sealing off every valve and vent while setting the proper levels. There were ten adjustments in all. Each controlled a different aspect of the fusing process. It had to be perfect: temperature, pressure, moisture, air quality, and time, along with five others that Carly had no idea what they meant. The gauges were marked: Klipton, Argonization, Fendehn, Upper (and Lower) Emplifier, and Hission. She figured she had no idea how the process worked, so why question? All she did was follow the instructions and hope she was operating the machine correctly.

When all was set, she glanced to the others and said, "Here goes nothing."

She hit the button marked ENGAGE, and the machine went to work. There was some clattering and sounds of scraping coming from behind the solid steel doors, but it was no more dramatic than any of the dry runs she had done.

"What exactly is it doing?" Dash asked Chris.

"It's breaking the tooth down to its base elemental form," Chris replied. "Those chemicals will eventually fuse with the other five elements we collect to create the Source."

The process took five minutes. The machine shut down and the green COMPLETE light illuminated.

"You going to take it out?" Gabriel asked.

"No," Carly replied. "It stays in the Element Fuser until the other five elements are added. But we can see what it looks like."

They stepped to the first of the smaller doors with the glass front. Everyone peered inside. A silver container moved forward on a conveyer belt until it stopped in front of the window.

"That's it?" Gabriel asked skeptically. "All that for a bowl of dust?"

"I guess so," Carly said, pointing to Chris.

Chris wore a big satisfied smile. He stared at the container of powder as if it held the most valuable gems to be found anywhere in the universe.

"That's it," Chris said. "Now on to step number two."

Twenty minutes later, the Alpha crew were strapped into their flight seats on the navigation deck. On the monitor was Chris, who was in his own flight seat in his quarters. Next to Chris was Rocket in a custom-made flight cage.

STEAM was attached to the rear wall of the navigation deck.

Gabriel had on his flight glasses.

"When we break out of orbit, we should be able to reconnect with Earth," Chris explained. "Shawn will be anxious to hear if we have been successful."

"Shawn?" Carly asked.

"Commander Phillips," Chris replied.

"I think our families would like to know too," Dash said.

"So where are we going, chief?" Gabriel said. "Time to give it up."

"The coordinates have been entered," Chris replied. "The next planet on our journey is called Meta Prime."

"Wait," Carly said. "I've heard that name before."

"Me too," Piper said. "It was that challenge at Base Ten with the robots and the machinery and the moving floor panels. Is that what we're going to face on Meta Prime?"

"Yes" was Chris's simple answer.

The crew exchanged anxious looks. This was not comforting news.

"I think I'd rather deal with dinosaurs," Gabriel said.

"We are approaching the orbital escape window," Chris announced.

Gabriel clicked back into pilot mode.

"Okay. Gamma drive is primed. Maximum booster load is pinned. We are ready to roll. Is everybody go?"

"Go."

"Go."

"Go."

"Steamer?" Gabriel called out.

"Let's go, yes sir!"

"All right! Brace for Gamma Speed in five . . . four . . . three . . . two . . . one . . . IGNITION."

Next stop, Meta Prime.

23

The tropical world of J-16 shrank in the rearview mirror of the *Cloud Leopard,* having been only momentarily disturbed by a visit from alien beings. Other than a Raptogon with a missing tooth, everything had returned to normal.

Almost.

The steady whir that was the sound of flying ZRKs broke the stillness of the tropical jungle. A swarm of six ZRKs flew in formation toward the new edge of the cliff that Chris had created with the *Cloud Cat.* Resting on the grass were the remains of the Raptogon tooth. The ZRKs circled the remnant, settled on top, observing.

They flew back to a sleek white craft that was perched on the cliff edge. It was the same size as the *Cloud Cat,* with a pointed nose and a tripod pedestal. Two doors on the top hinged open and the ZRKs entered.

There was a moment of total silence, and then an older boy emerged from the ship and made his way toward the Raptogon tooth.

Within an hour, the boy had returned, the engine whined

to life, and the craft lifted off. It floated out over the cliff, hung there a moment, then shot up to the sky.

Miles above the planet's surface, another spaceship was in orbit. It was a white ship, not unlike the smaller cargo craft. It looked like a flying wedge that began with a sharp nose and flared out into a triangle. It was at least as large as the *Cloud Leopard.* The smaller craft approached the giant ship and entered through an air lock in the stern.

On the navigation deck, a deck remarkably similar to the *Cloud Leopard*'s, four flight seats faced the center monitor. On the monitor was the same gray-haired man who had been observing the competition at Base Ten from deep inside the Sierra Nevada Mountains.

"I see the tooth has been secured," the man said. "It should be treated in the Element Fuser as quickly as possible. But first, you must be on your way. We don't want the *Cloud Leopard* to get too far ahead. Have you locked onto its Gamma trail?"

"Piece of cake," the pilot replied. "It'll be like following a trail of bread crumbs, just like we did to get here."

"Don't follow too closely," the man cautioned. "We don't want them to know they've got company . . . not yet, anyway. Bon voyage, *Light Blade.*"

The monitor went dark.

The pilot of the ship known as the *Light Blade* scanned the control panel on his seat, which was an exact duplicate of the control panel on the *Cloud Leopard.*

"Okay. Gamma drive is primed," he said, all business. "Maximum booster load is pinned. Time to fly. Is everybody go?"

"Go," replied Siena Moretti.

"Go," Niko Rodriguez said.

"Get us out of here," Anna Turner barked from the commander's seat. "I'm already sick of this place."

"All right!" Ravi Chavan said as he slipped on his flight glasses. "The Omega crew is outta here in four . . . three . . . two . . . one . . . IGNITION."

Anna gave a sly smile. "Here we come, Dash Conroy."

D. J. MacHale is the author of the bestselling series Pendragon: Journal of an Adventure Through Time and Space, the spooky Morpheus Road trilogy, and the sci-fi thriller trilogy The SYLO Chronicles. In addition to his published works, he has written, directed, and produced numerous award-winning television series and movies for young people, including *Are You Afraid of the Dark?*, *Flight 29 Down*, and *Tower of Terror*. D.J. lives with his family in Southern California. Visit him online at djmachalebooks.com.

NEXT DESTINATION:

META PRIME

When Team Alpha arrives on Meta Prime, they begin to search the metal planet for the molten lava they need. It should be easy: this planet is quiet. Even the native robots are frozen in time. But someone—or something—turns Meta Prime back on. . . .

SIGN ON. JOIN THE CREW. SAVE THE WORLD!

VOYAGERS

2

GAME OF FLAMES

ROBIN WASSERMAN

Each book contains hidden secrets and rewards. Unlock them all at:

VOYAGERSHQ.COM

The mission to save Earth is in YOUR hands.